Sin Is a Puppy

That Follows You Home

Sin Is a Puppy
That Follows You Home

by

BALARABA RAMAT YAKUBU

Translated from the Hausa by
ALIYU KAMAL

Published by

PUBLICATIONS
PRIVATE LIMITED

in association with

TRANQUEBAR

Blaft Publications Pvt. Ltd.
4/192 Ellaiamman Koil St.
Neelankarai
Chennai 600041 India
blaft.com

Tranquebar Press
Venkat Towers, 165, P.H. Road, Maduravoyal, Chennai 600095
No.38/10 (New No.5), Raghava Nagar, New Timber Yard Layout,
Bangalore 560026
Survey No. A-9, II Floor, Moula Ali Industrial Area, Moula Ali,
Hyderabad 500040
23/181, Anand Nagar, Nehru Road, Santacruz East, Mumbai 400055
47, Brij Mohan Road, Daryaganj, New Delhi 110002
westlandbooks.in

First published 1990 by Ramat General Enterprises as
Alhaki Kuykuyo Ne... © 1990 Balaraba Ramat Yakubu

First published in English by Blaft Publications in association with
Tranquebar Press 2012

English translation and all editorial content © 2011 Blaft Publications
All rights reserved.

ISBN 978-93-81626-84-9

Cover design: X.K.

A NOTE FROM THE PUBLISHERS

This book is, to the best of our knowledge, the first published English translation of a complete novel from Hausa, a language spoken by around 40 million people in several countries of West Africa. Hausa is written in two different scripts: a modified Arabic alphabet called *ajami*, used mostly for religious writings and poetry, and a modified Latin alphabet called *boko*, which emerged during the 19th century.

In the late 1980s, the northern Nigerian city of Kano was the centre of a boom in the publishing of Hausa fiction. Short novels began to appear, written in the *boko* script, printed cheaply, and aimed at a popular audience. They were stories of young love, stormy relationships, and family drama. The new genre came to be known as *littattafai na soyayya*, "love literature", or sometimes "Kano market literature". The latter name is often used pejoratively, by those who consider the novels to be vulgar. Some Hausa critics have called them a "corrupting influence"; others have even questioned the legality of the books under Islamic law. A less serious but not infrequent complaint is that the stories are derivative, and that the writers are too heavily influenced by Hindi films (which have been wildly popular among Hausa speakers for over half a century).

Hajiya Balaraba Ramat Yakubu, however, is undoubtedly an original. Starting out as the sole woman member of the pioneering Kano-based writer's club Raina Kama, she published her first book, *Budurwar Zuciya* ("Young at Heart"), in 1987. It was one of the earliest *soyayya* bestsellers. Three years later she published *Alhaki Kuykuyo Ne...*, her second novel, which cemented her reputation as one of the leading authors in the scene.

All of her nine novels have boldly addressed hot-button issues of Hausa society, including forced child marriage and the right to education for girls—issues with which Balaraba Ramat is intimately familiar, having been taken out of school herself to be married at the age of thirteen. Recently, she has gone on to tackle some of the same issues through the medium of film, working not only as a screenwriter, but also as director and producer.

In the early years of *soyayya* literature, women writers like Balaraba Ramat Yakubu and Bilkisu Ahmed Funtuwa were a minority. But things have changed: according to academic observers, women authors now dominate the field, and young women make up the bulk of the readership as well. The books are often credited as being partly responsible for the marked rise in literacy among Hausa women.

For all these reasons, we are delighted to have the chance to share Balaraba Ramat's work with a new audience via Dr. Aliyu Kamal's translation.

We have decided to present the book without a glossary. Very few Hausa words have been left untranslated, and of these, most can be understood from the context. (The words pertaining to Hausa cuisine are an exception, but English definitions like "porridge served with baobab-leaf soup" seem both clunky and woefully inadequate.)

However, a short note about Hausa titles may be helpful. The word *Hajiya*, used above to preface the author's name, indicates that she has completed the pilgrimage to Mecca; the masculine version, *Alhaji*, appears often in the book. In colloquial usage, *Alhaji* is sometimes applied to a man who can clearly afford to make the hajj, whether or not he has actually yet done so—it might signify only that he owns a car and dresses well. *Malam*, a modified form of the Arabic *mu'allim* ("teacher"), is another respectful title, but without the same connotation of wealth.

We would like to express our sincere gratitude to Gee Ameena Suleiman and Nisha Ravindranathan for their help with proof-reading and editing; Muhtar Bakare of the Lagos-based publishing house Kachifo Limited, who first turned us on to the world of Hausa popular fiction; Dr. Yusuf Adamu of the Association of Nigerian Authors; and especially Prof. Abdalla Uba Adamu of the University of Kano, without whose enthusiastic support and expert advice the project would never have come to fruition.

Rakesh Khanna
Blaft Publications
Chennai

PREFACE

In this book, I tell a story about a type of man found commonly in Nigeria who regards a married woman with children as a sort of slave to be bought or sold at the marketplace. These men think they may treat such a woman as poorly as they like, since they believe her to be completely worthless. They may be rich and comfortable themselves, yet refuse to feed and clothe their own families—while simultaneously denying anyone else the right to do so.

Such men fail to heed the hadith of Prophet Muhammad: "Allah will bless the efforts of those charged with the divine responsibility of caring for others." They are arrogant on account of being privileged, and they only provide for their families as and when it suits their personal capricious whims. Their wives are forced to work and trade in order to make ends meet and to keep their children from having to go about naked. Men who behave this way clearly never spare a thought for the hereafter, or else they would not perpetrate their evil deeds. There are even those among them who are so irreverent that, when people dare to admonish them, they simply shrug the warnings aside, saying that the hereafter won't come any time soon.

Perhaps, they are thinking of the hadith that says that a woman's salvation is tied up with the salvation of her husband. But it is not only in the hereafter that Allah deals with men like this. No, Allah deals with each person as his or her own deeds warrant.

In this story, He deals with the character I have named "Alhaji Abdu" by demonstrating that whenever one person's rights are infringed upon by another, He is a witness.

I hope my story will serve as a lesson to the Muslim community. May the Lord God make the sinners change their ways, as He does not forgive a man's crime against another.

I am deeply grateful to Allah for giving me the inspiration to write this novel.

Hajiya Balaraba Ramat Yakubu
Marubuciya

CHAPTER ONE

Alhaji Abdu was a small business owner with a stall at Sabon Gari Market. He sold fabrics, cotton prints, and headscarves. Though he rarely had enough stock to fill the stall, the merchandise still amounted to about one hundred thousand naira. Some of his merchandise was received from a supplier, but he owned about one-third of it himself. He was very well known in the market, not least because his stall was always filled with female customers, with whom he flirted shamelessly.

He was married with children, but his wife, Rabi, had no control over him. He was constantly after other women. At least Rabi could console herself with the fact that he didn't marry and divorce his women friends at will; only once, after they had been married ten years, had he married a second wife. That woman had borne him a daughter, but had later left him, abandoning the child, because he would not stop chasing women.

Alhaji Abdu had now been married to Rabi for twenty-two years. She had borne him nine children: six boys and three girls. So far, these children had kept her from deserting his house—but that seemed fated to happen eventually, for he treated her as badly as it is possible for a man to treat his wife. She had suffered for it, as was plain for all to see; she had an emaciated look, and went about in clothes that were hardly better than rags.

They lived in the *bakin kasuwa*, the district of Kano city around the circular market, and shared their walls with neighbours who could hear everything that was said in the house—a fact that the neighbours were surely not very happy about. Their clothesline was made from bits of cloth tied together, and an open drain ran through the middle of the house. In the courtyard, where the cooking was done, the smoke that billowed out from the wood stove had blackened all the walls. Rabi cooked in the courtyard because her husband had filled the kitchen with junk, and insisted on keeping it locked. In the rainy season she had no alternative but to cook in the second entranceway. She was terribly burdened with work, and was always found either holding a broom, or doing the dishes at the tap, or cooking food at the hearth to sell.

Alhaji Abdu was never much help. He never even did as much as buy them ingredients for soup. He would simply distribute fifty kobo each to Rabi and the children and let them fend for themselves for breakfast and lunch. But to his mother, who lived with them, he would give one whole naira. He'd also give Rabi five naira to buy meat, Maggi cubes, salt and soup ingredients for the evening meal. There was plenty of corn, at least; whenever that ran out, he would buy another sack.

But Alhaji Abdu had no idea whether the food his wife cooked was tasty or not, because he always ate out at hotels. He rarely returned home before midnight. He never even had breakfast at home in the mornings, let alone lunch. His room always remained locked through the day until he came back home. Once in a while, when it became untidy, he would call one of his children to sweep it for him; otherwise, no one was allowed inside.

His wife used to watch him put on expensive clothes sewed from brocade, and spray himself with pleasant perfumes, the scent of which would linger in the house long after he had gone out. Yet he never bothered to buy simple soap and detergent for her and the children. He did buy new clothes for the boys for the festivals of Sallah Karama and Sallah Babba; sometimes on a sudden whim he would include shoes and caps as well. As for the girls, they would each get a six-yard *atamfa* cotton print with a matching veil—but not the money to cover the tailoring charges. Rabi and Alhaji Abdu's mother would get the same. These were the only times that the members of the family ever felt any joy, for they would receive nothing at all from him until the following year.

Alhaji Abdu, on the other hand, never kept any one set of clothes longer than three months. In the morning he would go out and spend five naira on gourmet dishes with boiled eggs, and for lunch there was a food-seller woman who knew how to cook to his taste. For three naira, she would send spaghetti with yams and meat over to his fabric stall, with a bottled soft drink to wash the food down. Sometimes, he would buy five naira worth of roast tripe from a passing seller, and feast on that as well. Then, at night, he would eat at the Kano Tourist Hotel, spending another four or five naira. After the meal, he would look for somewhere to relax. If he had a woman friend lined up, he would go to her place. Otherwise he would start looking for a new catch, and if he got lucky, he would spend the night with her. Only if all his efforts to secure a woman for the night failed would he end up back with Rabi, who often went up to three months at a stretch without spending a single night with her husband. Even when Alhaji Abdu did come home, Rabi often declined to sleep with him, because she thought he wouldn't enjoy being with her.

It was this attitude of Alhaji Abdu towards his family that forced his wife to get into the food-selling business. In the morning, she would prepare *koko* and fry *kosai*; aside from what was sold, she would keep some for her and her children to eat as well. At lunchtime, she would cook rice and yams, and make *gurasa*, and they would eat some of that too. At sunset, she would cook *tuwo* with *miyan kuka*. All this cooking gave her some distraction from her miserable home life; and besides the profits generated from the business, she was able to feed her children.

Five of her children attended primary school, one was in secondary school, and the youngest two stayed at home. She cared for them all, including the eldest of the nine, her son Kabiru, who had just finished secondary school and was looking for a job. She had bought their school books and uniforms and paid all their school fees, slowly selling off her belongings—including the enamel-ware *kwalla*, *fanteka*, and serving dishes that her family had given her when she was married—until her room became bare. In the past, she had always managed to keep a sack of rice and a sack of corn in store, but lately it seemed that all the proceeds from her daily trade were spent on the kids.

She persevered without protest, because whenever she tried to complain to Alhaji Abdu about the family's plight it led to an awful shouting match that all the neighbours could hear. When her daughter Saudatu got admission into a secondary school, and Rabi listed out to her husband all the supplies that needed to be bought for the girl, he became so incensed that he spoke the word *talaq*, pronouncing a separation, and sent Rabi from the house. It wasn't the demand for school supplies that infuriated him so much as Rabi's firm and repeated insistence, during their argument, that after death would come a day of judgement. Rabi went home to her mother, and told her everything; but in the end her mother had her taken back to Alhaji Abdu's house. She couldn't let Rabi stay, what with all the children clinging to her.

Rabi's mother was compelled to sell a big ram that she owned to pay for all her granddaughter's school supplies. The old woman worked as a food-seller as well, making bean-cakes in the morning and *alkubus* and vegetable soup for lunch. Besides Rabi she had a son, Malam Shehu, who was a civil servant, and a daughter, Tasidi, who was a housewife. Rabi's husband earned more than her sister's, but Tasidi's life was far more comfortable. Both Rabi's siblings pitied her, and helped her financially. They knew she had too many children to walk out on her husband. If she did leave, where would she take them? Who would they stay with? The sorry state of her circumstances meant that she had no alternative but to remain in the house of Alhaji Abdu.

Rabi's eldest sons Kabiru and Ibrahim, and her eldest daughter Saudatu (who had recently come of age), understood how unhappy their father made life for their mother; they also realized that she was the one who took responsibility for all their needs. As a result, they always took her side in any dispute. They never complained to her about anything, never disagreed with anything she said, never disobeyed her. The same was true of the younger ones. The more their father mistreated Rabi, the more her children supported her through good behaviour and kindness.

One day, without warning, Rabi's mother died. The giant wall that had protected Rabi had crashed to the ground; the tree that had shaded her and her children had burnt to ashes. Among her siblings, Rabi was the most distraught, and she and her children grieved the hardest. Everybody sympathized with her plight. After forty days, whatever little property the old woman had left was distributed among her children—twelve sheep, a thousand naira in cash, and some plates and dishes she had put away to give as a gift for Saudatu's wedding. Malam Shehu took for himself only a single ram, to slaughter at the naming ceremony of the child he was expecting any day now. His sisters shared everything else; Tasidi took an ewe with two kids, two wraps, and a veil to remember her mother by, and left the rest with Rabi. Their mother's house was refurbished and rented out, while the animals—with the exception of the one that Tasidi took to raise—were sold. The proceeds of the sale, which came to 1000 naira, were deposited in a bank under Rabi's name. Rabi warned Kabiru never to tell anyone about the bank account, not even Malam Shehu or Tasidi.

Alhaji Abdu did not pay attention to any of this. He seemed to have changed a little during the mourning period, leading people to wonder whether he had finally taken a turn for the better, especially when they saw his car parked outside his house during the daytime. Rabi thanked God that her husband had turned over a new leaf; he began bringing meat home, and sometimes Omo detergent and bathing soap. He even bought her an atamfa cloth. Rabi's skin began to regain some of its glow.

Though no one would ever call her beautiful, Rabi was tall and had a good figure. She was energetic, yet soft spoken. She only argued with her husband when there was a good reason for it. Alhaji Abdu's mother had often praised Rabi's patience and good manners, saying that nobody else on earth would put up with her son the way his wife did. It was his mother's way of trying to make him see reason; but her words never seemed to have an effect on him. After years of this, she had lost her patience with him, and stopped returning his greetings. When that didn't seem to bother him, she resorted to asking his uncles to talk to him. But he never listened to them either.

Malam Ibrahim, Alhaji Abdu's father, had been famous for his friendly nature and generosity and had provided well for his family, but Alhaji Abdu did not take after him. On the contrary, all his blood relatives shunned his house. No one ever went there to ask any favour out of fear of being treated with contempt. Although Alhaji Abdu was the eldest, it was his younger brother, Alhaji Bello, who attended to needy relatives. Whenever one of their sisters had a falling out with her husband, she would prefer to go to Alhaji Bello's house.

During the brief change that came over him, Alhaji Abdu gave his house a lick of paint and covered the drain. He even cleaned out all his junk from the kitchen and had the stoves put back inside.

The reason for the change? Alhaji Abdu was planning to take another wife. But he kept his mouth shut about it. He simply gave the house a sprucing up and filled the kitchen with sacks of food.

This surprised Rabi a great deal. Her husband had never done so much as bring a sack of rice to the house before, but here he was returning home before the Asr prayer, smiling cheerfully and clutching a bag of money. Before, he had always come home looking angry, snubbing anyone who welcomed him and kicking aside anything he saw in his way. Now, when he asked his children about their day at school, they were speechless with surprise, never having heard him ask questions like that before.

They kept staring at him as he passed them on his way to his room. After resting inside for some time, he brought out from his bag an atamfa cloth, a blouse, a headscarf, a veil, six bars of soap, two bottles of pomade, and twenty naira, and called for Rabi.

He had to wait while she had a bath. As he waited for her, he thought over the manner in which he ran his home, which had attracted comment from everyone. He blamed Rabi for discussing their private matters with the neighbours. No one would know of the conditions in which he kept his family if she had not told them. But everything would change for the better, now that he was going to take a second wife. He felt he would finally be able to relax at home again, without the children always bothering him.

The new wife, Delu, was thirty-eight years old, and had never borne any children. She was, in fact, a former prostitute who had been married twice in the past. The first marriage was to an old man from whom no bride-price had been collected. She was hardened even then, and she didn't stay married for more than a year. She was working as a prostitute when she met the man who became her second husband. That marriage lasted for five years, until the husband realized that Delu was sneaking out to meet other men. At first, he wouldn't listen to what people said about her, but then his senior wife told him that even his own younger brother was among Delu's lovers. The senior wife even promised to show him proof.

It so happened that two days later, the man's brother came back from the village where he lived and worked. Once every fortnight, this brother used to leave his wife and children in the village and come to his brother's house for the weekend. He stayed in a room with a door that opened onto the entranceway, so you had to pass it on your way in or out. People had already noticed how his brother's wife used to cook him elaborate dishes, but they had assumed it was just hospitality. That night, the senior wife stayed awake until well after midnight when finally she heard Delu go out through the entranceway. She followed Delu, and watched her go into the brother's room and close the door. She told her husband about it the following day, and that night he too stayed awake and witnessed Delu sneaking out. Angrily, he made as if to follow her, but his first wife stopped him. They roused everyone in the house and went to his brother's room, where Delu's husband violently kicked the door open. He switched on the light—and caught his brother with Delu, like a mortar in a pestle.

That was the end of Delu's second marriage.

Anger and shame forced her to flee to Lagos. She had been there for sixteen years, wandering from one place to another, until just six months ago, when she had returned to Kano.

Alhaji Abdu had first met Delu when she came to his stall to buy atamfa cloth. She still had some glow of youth left to show off, and she still had some naira in her handbag. By the end of the transaction, he had fallen in love with her—in fact, he ended up giving her the cloth free of charge. He kept chatting with her until after the Asr prayer, so that he could take her home in his car and see where she lived. Less than seven days later, during which time he spent lavishly on her, he began talking of marriage. She lied that she had no belongings, saying that her former husband in Lagos had refused to allow her to take her things after their divorce. She eventually gave in to Alhaji Abdu's proposal of marriage when he promised to buy for her everything that she might need. He purchased a lot of expensive furniture—a bed, a mattress, a wardrobe, a dressing table, and two chairs—as well as linoleum for her room, three rolls of atamfa cloth, and headscarves and veils of lace and silk. In addition to all this, he also gave her one hundred naira to buy whatever else she wanted.

The bedroom set alone had cost Alhaji Abdu not less than four hundred and fifty naira. God alone knew how much he had spent altogether. He and Delu had fixed the date for the wedding, and planned that she would move into the house that same day. Now it was the day before the wedding, and Alhaji Abdu was about to announce to Rabi his decision to take a second wife. He had brought her gifts, as was the custom.

||

CHAPTER TWO

||

"As patient as a dabb lizard"—that was how they used to describe Saudatu Abdu at school. Unlike most of her friends, she had never been sent to the principal for fighting; she was always calm and well-behaved. The girl was in her fifth and final year of school, and in that whole time, she had not once been caught breaking a rule, or even accused of anything. She would eat whatever was served up from the school kitchen without complaint, garnishing the food with nothing but ground pepper.

As she got ready to return to school after the holidays, all she had to take with her was a measure of cassava flour, some *kuli-kuli*, four bars of soap, two packets of detergent, and five naira. She made no complaint or protest, though, since she was aware that it was her mother who had bought everything for her. Rabi had paid the twenty naira school fee for her daughter, as well. Once, it had happened that all of Saudatu's stores had been stolen from her dormitory room, but even then the incredibly uncomplaining girl hadn't sent home for more, trusting in God that He would see her through. Her friends had helped her out until the next holidays.

Aside from her resilience, it was her devotion to religion that most impressed her friends. She went to the school mosque four times a day, every day; only for the Subhi prayer would she stay in her dormitory to pray. The imam soon took notice of her on account of her punctuality. She was the first to carry out any special prayers that he asked them to say, and she never missed the voluntary *tarawi* prayers during the fasting of Ramadan.

One day, the imam gave them a very difficult prayer to conduct, explaining that Allah would listen to the wishes of anyone who carried out the prayer as they were asked to. Saudatu and her friends all promised to do it, but when none of the other girls showed any inclination to fulfil the promise, she bathed and went to the mosque alone. In the end, she beseeched Allah with a simple request: to bless her with a good, upright husband, and to bless her mother Rabi with wealth.

That night, Saudatu had a startling, vivid dream. She saw herself praying in a very high building while her friends watched her from below. They thought she would fall, but she didn't. When she related the dream to the imam, he seemed surprised, even though the girl told him that she had said the prayer as instructed. He advised her to give some alms, and not to tell anyone else about the dream.

She scrimped and saved and bought some groundnuts and doled them out to her friends. At the time, they were all about to write their second-to-last set of exams, just before the end-of-the-year holidays. Her friends had assumed the reason she was giving out alms was that she hoped for good luck on the exams. When she had first joined the school, she hadn't seemed very bright; they remembered that she had gotten rather poor grades her first year, only managing to rank twentieth out of a class of thirty-five.

Saudatu's brother Kabiru had given her a sound beating for her poor performance that first year, and their mother had had to step in to save her from further punishment. Kabiru had threatened to take her out of school and marry her off. This ordeal seemed to pay off, though, for in her second year, Saudatu began to get better grades. Soon, Hadiza Sulaiman, Saudatu Abdu and Bara'atu Manzo were counted as the brightest girls in the class. Hadiza always came first, retaining her position at the top, with the other two vying for second place. So far, in her fifth year, Saudatu had been at best the second and at worst the third, never once slipping to fourth. It so happened that in this set of exams, after the prayer and the dream, she achieved the first rank for the first time since she had joined the school.

She sent home a very long letter about the exam results, and telling Kabiru about attaining the first rank. Rabi, of course, was overjoyed with her daughter's success.

CHAPTER THREE

|||

Rabi walked out of the bathroom and had just started putting on her makeup when Bilkisu, her second-oldest daughter, came in to tell her that her husband wanted to see her.

She quickly dressed up and went to him.

"*Salamu alaikum,*" she said. "I was told you wanted to see me."

"Aha, the Senior Wife," he said jocularly. "I have something to tell you. I plan to take a second wife. Here; these are the gifts normally given on making the announcement."

Rabi was struck dumb; she simply couldn't think of anything to say to him. How strange! Their daughter was old enough to be married, and he hadn't even begun making preparations. Instead, here he was making plans to take another wife for himself.

When she didn't reply, Alhaji Abdu thought it was because she was feeling jealous. He said, "If these gifts are not sufficient, say so, and I will bring you more. Why are you so angry? Why are you acting like someone just died?"

She glared at him and said, "Take ten new wives if you want. I don't care what gifts you bring to announce it." Gesturing towards the things, she went on, "I'd rather see you buy some bedsheets for Saudatu's wedding, than bring me ten atamfa cloths."

"What do you mean? Don't you like the things?"

"No, I thank you for them. But you should marry off your daughter before you marry yourself."

"Listen, now: My marriage will take place today and my new wife will join me here tomorrow. As for Saudatu, I never said I wouldn't marry her off. She just has to attract a suitable husband."

"Is this woman you're marrying a virgin or a divorcee?" she asked, then continued before he could answer: "And I suppose that's why you've being going to all this expense recently, so that your new bride will be impressed with how well you look after your home?"

"What senseless talk. You mean to say I don't look after my household?"

"You know you don't," Rabi retorted. "When did you last buy us a sack of rice? How much do you give us to prepare meals? How much do you give us to buy break fast, for that matter?"

"Now you're making ridiculous accusations, just because I want to marry again. This is your underhanded way of trying to keep her from moving into my house."

"Allah is witness to all that you've done to me. May He bless the marriage, but may He do so only after you change your ways."

Rabi went out without collecting the gifts. Before she entered her room, he called to her, "There is something else. Hear me out."

She went back and sat before him quietly.

"Listen carefully," he said, pointing a finger at her. "Don't you dare let my new bride hear you talk this way when she comes into this house. And furthermore, don't let people put the idea into your head that just because I have so many children with you, I can't divorce you. It's not true. Things have changed. We can part ways even now. So watch out."

She looked at him for a few seconds before leaving the room again, shedding tears. She wept for a long time in her room, unable to understand what her husband meant about things having changed. Was it because her mother had died or because he was about to remarry?

There wasn't enough time for Rabi to invite many people to the wedding. She could only invite her sister, her brother's wife, and her friend Salamatu to keep her company on the day the new bride joined the family.

The bride arrived and settled in with all the hauteur of a princess. She spent a week sharing Alhaji Abdu's bed, during which time she took it upon herself to prepare three full meals a day for him on her own. Later, even after that first week, when Rabi and the new bride began to take turns, Alhaji Abdu refused to eat the food Rabi cooked. It seemed he now felt that only Delu knew how to cook to his taste. When Rabi could no longer tolerate his treatment, she began to complain, but it was no use.

Even Alhaji Abdu's mother got tired of complaining, and eventually she gave up too, just as Rabi had. They watched while Alhaji Abdu and Delu carried on shamelessly. Alhaji Abdu stuck to Delu as if she was the only woman he had ever married. All the rights that Rabi should have enjoyed as a wife—even the right to share her bed with him—were disregarded.

And yet Rabi continued her work as a good mother. She went on raising Ladidi, the daughter who had been left behind by Alhaji Abdu's former wife, alongside her own daughter Bilkisu, who was about the same age, loving and caring for them equally. She would buy matching things for them, like earrings, so that people who saw them often mistook them for twins. She had been doing this ever since Ladidi was only two; she was now eleven.

One day, though, Delu persuaded her husband that Ladidi should be taken away from Rabi's care and turned over to her to raise. When Alhaji Abdu's mother heard about this and objected, he answered, "Inna, Delu has no children to look after; she's lonely. And you know how Ladidi is suffering at the hands of..."

"*La'ilaha illallahu!* There is no god but Allah," his mother interrupted. "What a hypocrite you are! Be mindful of Rabi's rights. You're courting hellfire. If Ladidi is really suffering so much, why didn't you take her away before? Be careful, don't stir up a fight."

"By Allah, Inna, she'll find life more comfortable if Delu looks after her..."

"If you won't do the right thing, then get out of my sight. Go on then, treat that woman however you damn please—but beware of the day when Allah will come to her aid. Now leave."

But all her warnings fell on deaf ears. As the eloquent among the Hausa people say, a man who has gone far away doesn't hear when he is called.

Life went on in this way until, without much warning, Alhaji Abdu's mother breathed her last. She went down with diarrhoea one night and died the next morning at dawn. Her last words before death were spoken to her son, concerning Rabi: "Abdu, Rabi is more than a wife to you. You must treat her as your blood. In the name of Allah and His Prophet, take care of her; be a friend to her; place your trust in her. Think of the children you've had together."

Those parting words were her last-ditch attempt to improve the relations between Rabi and Alhaji Abdu. But it didn't take many days after her death until he was back to his old ways. In fact, now that there was nobody left to keep him in check, his conduct became even worse than before.

News of the marriage and the death were not relayed to Saudatu at school until she came home for the holidays. She was informed of the marriage right at the entrance to the house by Bilkisu, and met Delu in the family compound. Saudatu felt an instant dislike towards this woman, her father's new wife; and for her part, Delu decided right then that among Alhaji Abdu's children, she hated Saudatu most bitterly of all. She glared at the girl for a moment, then went back to chopping lettuce for her husband, who liked to eat lettuce with powdered peanuts as an accompaniment to every dish placed before him.

Saudatu found her mother sitting on the floor of her room with her legs spread apart, preparing chillies for the soup. Rabi looked up and was surprised by how grown-up her daughter looked next to the other children who followed her in.

"Saudatu, so you're home for the holidays? Welcome back," her mother said.

"*Baba,* you look thin," said Saudatu. "Have you been sick?"

"I am fine, Saudatu. Although I'm suffering from heartache."

"Where is Inna? Is she in her room?"

Rabi couldn't answer her, knowing that the girl hadn't been told of the old woman's death. Immediately, her son Mustapha piped up: "Inna has died."

Saudatu burst into tears and was soon joined by her brothers and sisters. Rather than trying to stop them, Rabi joined in herself. They were still at it when the head of the household came home.

Upon hearing the cries, he asked Delu, "What's going on in there? What happened, Delu?"

"Don't ask me, Alhaji," said Delu. "Ask your goat of a wife! Ask her why she calls the children together and tries to fill the whole house with their wailing!"

He took her side at once, and instead of asking Rabi the problem, he went to her room in a huff and said, "This is so stupid of you. Why collect all the children here and then join them in a crying match? When will you grow up?"

"Will you call me an animal, too, like your old whore of a wife just did?" Rabi asked.

"She was right to call you an animal, seeing as how foolish you're being!"

Delu joined them then; she had heard what Rabi had called her, and wanted to give her something back. "You bitch! Calling me an old whore—what do you think *you* are? What have you done with your life? You're completely and totally worthless."

"I am *not* worthless." Rabi rose to her feet. "You used-up piece of trash, you're lucky this man pitied you enough to marry you. Shrivelled useless bitch! Look, he might encourage you to abuse people, but as for me, I'm fed up with you. If you dare insult me again, I won't show you any mercy."

"You dare call me a piece of trash?" yelled Delu. "You'll pay for saying that! I'll break your bones!"

In the blink of an eye, right in front of Alhaji Abdu, the women began to wrestle. He tried to get in between them to separate them, but Rabi's children, on hearing the commotion, rushed to her defence and descended on Delu with their fists. Alhaji Abdu tried to stop them, but he was completely outnumbered. The moment he pulled one child away, another would rush in to deal Delu another blow. If Delu managed to hit away the boys or girls, Rabi would punch her again. This went on until Rabi got the upper hand and threw Delu to the ground. As soon as she fell down, Saudatu sat on her and rained more blows on her. Rabi kept pummelling her as well, as hard as she could. Alhaji Abdu tried to lift Saudatu off of Delu so Delu could get back on her feet, but Rabi shouted, "Don't let her up, Saudatu! Give her the thrashing she deserves! Delu, today you'll see what a virtue it is to bear children. Try to take Ladidi away from me, will you? She's not your daughter, you bitch!"

"Have you gone mad?" demanded Alhaji Abdu. "Are you trying to kill her? Useless people. Get off her, Saudatu!"

He finally managed to pull the girl off of Delu, who burst into tears the moment she got to her feet. "Wayyo Allah, I have come to grief! You've all ganged up to kill me! By God, I will not stay in this house. They tried to murder me right before your very eyes and you act like you don't even care. Wayyo Allah!"

Alhaji Abdu knew that if Delu left now, he would never be able to bring her back. He loved her, and he was ready to divorce Rabi to keep her.

"What a waste it is for a man to marry a prostitute," Rabi was saying to Delu. "Better he can just have his share and then leave. Go now, find someone else who wants a share of you."

That was the last straw for Alhaji Abdu. He raised his hand and gave Rabi a mighty slap. Just at that moment, Kabiru entered the room. He saw Rabi fall to the floor from the force of the blow. Oblivious to the boy, Alhaji Abdu was about to whack her again when he felt someone catch hold of his arm. He turned around to see Kabiru, who asked, "What's the matter, father? What wrong has she done to you?"

"I didn't realize this cursed mother of yours was such a raving lunatic," he said. "This bitch and her children pounced on an innocent woman and beat her up. By God, I ought to divorce her!"

"Come on, Baba, this isn't a matter for divorce," said Kabiru. "Please calm down."

"If you want to divorce me because of this poor old hag, then *bismilla*, go right ahead," said Rabi. "But she only married you for your money, so don't be surprised if she runs off before too long."

"You're the one fated to live the life of a poor old hag," said Delu to Rabi. "For God's sake, just look at you."

"Well, that's hardly as bad a fate as being married to a whore," Rabi said. No sooner had the words had left her mouth than Delu rushed over and slapped her.

Kabiru, seeing that his father wasn't going to do anything about it, became furious, and gave Delu a slap with the palm of his hand—so forcefully that she was thrown to the ground.

"You detestable boy!" shouted his father. "Why did you strike her? Get out of my house! From today, I will have nothing more to do with you!"

"He's not going anywhere," said Rabi, "and if you try to make him, we'll all go with him."

"I divorce you," Alhaji Abdu told Rabi. "We are no longer man and wife. Take your children and leave my house. I am finished with all of you."

"And do you think we'll be ruined? You think these children will die because you disowned them? Remember, Allah blesses his servants by enriching them. He will bless these children as well. You go on enjoying your money; we don't need it."

"Get all your things together and leave my house right now," he ordered. Then he turned to Delu, who was standing in a corner snivelling. "You... Go to your room."

"You've poured your water on the ground, now you can lap it up," Rabi said to her, quoting a proverb. "You've got what you wanted: he has thrown me and all of his children out of his house. Congratulations. Now you had better go pay your witch doctor for helping you pull it off."

"*Alhamdu lillahi*, thanks and praise to Allah," said Delu. "Your association with this house is over. And good riddance! Now you can go sit with your memories."

By the time Rabi got to her room, she was so distraught she could hardly see straight. The first thing she did was to send Kabiru to her sister Tasidi's house. Then she and Saudatu went to Malam Shehu's house to tell him what had happened. The other children, who had already come back from the Qur'anic school, had to be left at home. By the time of the afternoon Asr prayers, all of Rabi's relatives had heard about the sad developments.

Malam Shehu rushed over to Alhaji Abdu's younger brother, Alhaji Bello, with the news. He and Alhaji Bello agreed to go and see Rabi's husband after the sunset Magrib prayer to discuss the problem and see whether man and wife could be reconciled.

From there, Malam Shehu went to Tasidi's house, only to be told that she had already left for *his* house. Luckily, though, Tasidi's husband, Alhaji Sule, was at home; he agreed to accompany Malam Shehu and Alhaji Bello to the house of Alhaji Abdu that evening. Having made all these arrangements, Malam Shehu went back home.

Later, when they all arrived at Alhaji Abdu's house and sent in word of their arrival, Alhaji Abdu knew what was afoot.

Delu, too, guessed that efforts were being made to bring Rabi back to the house, and she was determined to put a stop to it. As her husband got up to go and meet the callers, she said to him, "They're here to plead on Rabi's behalf. You'll have to choose between her and me. By Allah, I won't go on living in the same house as her, not after the way she insulted me."

"Who said I was going to bring her back? Don't you bother about all this."

"Look at them, all ganging up and coming here. There's no one here to stand up for me."

"I'll stand up for you," Alhaji Abdu replied. "It's done: I have divorced her. If one of them thinks I'm under some special obligation to take her back, he had better let me know."

Alhaji Abdu took more than fifteen minutes before coming out to meet his visitors, and when he finally emerged, he was wearing the pompous frown of a prince about to face a group of prisoners begging for clemency. The visitors ignored the look on his face, and once they had all exchanged greetings, Alhaji Bello said to him, "Today Malam Shehu has informed me about a most unfortunate incident. One shouldn't end a marriage because of a quarrel between women."

"One can't avoid something that is fated to happen," said Alhaji Abdu. "Allah has decreed that the marriage should end."

"But Alhaji, when quarrels like this happen, one must exercise patience," said Tasidi's husband, Alhaji Sule. "People no longer bother much about womens' arguments these days. Please, let us bring Rabi back. Reconsider your decision, at least for the sake of your children."

"Now listen!" shouted Alhaji Abdu. "I refuse to be treated as some powerless nobody in my own house. Do you realize that Rabi and her children ganged up on my second wife and beat her up, for no reason whatsoever, despite all my efforts to stop them? Am I supposed to give up all authority over them?"

Malam Shehu let Alhaji Abdu calm known for a moment, then said, "From what my sister told me, the incident was not serious enough to warrant a divorce."

Alhaji Abdu answered by telling them exactly what had transpired, leaving nothing out. When he was done, Alhaji Bello said, "If that's true, then Kabiru isn't to blame. You beat his mother to protect your second wife. Then your second wife beat his mother in your presence, but you didn't do anything. I don't think it was wrong for him to protect his own mother."

"That's your own view," said Alhaji Abdu.

"The best thing to do," said Alhaji Sule, "is to let the matter rest. Forgive her and take her back. May Allah prevent any future trouble."

"I have already divorced her," said Alhaji Abdu. "I will have nothing more to do with her."

"Oh, come on, Alhaji," said Alhaji Bello. "Don't say that. It isn't right for you to just ignore all our advice like this."

"What, is there some debt I owe to one of you for marrying her to me? No, this doesn't concern any of you. I will not take her back. She can keep the children, I don't want them."

"You're being rash in your judgement," said Alhaji Bello, "and it is not very becoming of you. What's come over you? At least after Inna's death you should have started to see reason. Remember, that's how this whole thing started: Saudatu came back home from school and burst into tears on being told of her grandmother's death, and then everyone started crying. That's how attached she was to your own mother. Isn't that right, Alhaji Sule?"

"This thing is beyond me," said Alhaji Sule, getting up. "You're his blood relative, maybe you'll have better luck getting him to listen. I may as well go. See you later, Malam Shehu."

Malam Shehu got up too, and said to Alhaji Abdu, "You should remember that even while you and Rabi were together, we were the ones who took responsibility for her welfare and that of her children. You may have disowned them now, but we will continue to look after them. May the children grow up and be blessed by Allah. May He see to it that they and Rabi receive what is their due. Farewell."

Alhaji Sule and Malam Shehu left, leaving Alhaji Bello alone with his brother, looking deeply distressed. Finally, after a few minutes of silence, he asked him, "So you think you have handled this matter well? Do you really think so, Alhaji Abdu?"

"Have I done anything so strange?" Alhaji Abdu protested. "I'm not the first person who has ever divorced his wife. What's so unthinkable about it?"

"And how many children do you have? She bore you nine! Death would be more honourable than divorce! You know she does everything she can to feed and clothe those children. Think it over, and beware of what fate may have in store for you. Show some consideration and take back your wife."

"By Allah, I will not," said Alhaji Abdu. "I am finished with her. And I'm fed up with all this endless talk. Get out of my sight."

"You are just like the Pharaoh: people have apologized to you, but you refuse to listen to them. So be it. From today, you and I are through. By Allah, if you so much as try to approach my body at my funeral, I'll hold it against you."

As Alhaji Bello rose to go, his brother said, "So what if we are through? I don't depend on you for my food or my clothing. I earned my money without your help. What do I have to lose by parting ways with you? I'm finished with you as well. You can forget that I ever existed."

Alhaji Bello had walked out of the house without waiting to listen to this whole speech, but now he turned back, and said, "All that money you're so proud of is really worth nothing. Allah can take it all away in a flash. A man who doesn't understand the virtues of marriage can never appreciate God's true blessings. As for you, one can hardly even call you a Muslim."

"Go then. Go pray to Allah to make you rich and make me poor. I really don't care what you do."

"I'm comfortable as I am, you stupid idiot."

And with that they parted, feeling nothing but loathing for each other. Just as the twenty-year marriage of Rabi and Alhaji Abdu had ended, so had the relationship between the two brothers.

Rabi hired a truck and packed all her belongings in it. At first, she had planned to take only her two youngest children with her, but when she and the women who had helped her pack got into the truck, the other children began howling uncontrollably. Shouting and crying, the boys climbed onto the truck, while Saudatu ran up and down in a frenzy, until she fell and began rolling on the ground in tears. Rabi had no choice but to squeeze them all into the truck beside her. The eldest, Kabiru, had not yet come back from Tasidi's, and his brother, Ibrahim, was still away at school.

Rabi took the children to the house of Malam Shehu, who was speechless when he saw them. The whole situation was making him feel as heartsick as if Death itself had come calling.

"The best thing you can do for me," Rabi told him, "is to find me a house on rent. I can't stay here with all these kids. It would be too much for your wife and children; with such a crowded house, we'd all end up quarrelling every day. Besides, my boys and girls have been attending the Shahuci Primary School and Malam Hadi's Qur'anic School. If we move all the way over here, they'll have to transfer to new schools, and it will disrupt their education. So for the sake of Allah and His Prophet, find me a house to rent not too far from our old one, where I can continue with my food-selling business. That's the only thing to be done."

Malam Shehu sympathized with her and appreciated the concern she voiced about staying in his house. If there was a falling out between Rabi and his wife, it could seriously damage his own relationship with his sister. And he knew that just as it is impossible to avoid accidentally biting one's tongue with one's teeth once in a while, it is equally impossible to prevent women from quarrelling.

So, Malam Shehu began to make enquiries, and three days later he found two bedrooms in a house in Rimin Kira. There were three other tenants in the house: a hospital staff worker, his wife, and a young bachelor. Rabi moved into one room with the girls, and let the boys take the other room.

She started cooking and selling food at once, and thankfully her fare was in constant demand. Business increased until she was cooking up to five *mudu* measures of rice every day, along with yams, macaroni, and beans. Schoolchildren, local people, and others from the surrounding areas all bought food from her. In the morning, she would cook *koko* porridge, which her children would eat with bean-cakes they bought from another neighbourhood seller. Before too long, Rabi had filled out, and started to look healthy again.

CHAPTER FOUR

||||

A week before she was to go back to school, Saudatu asked Rabi to let her go spend the day at her aunt Tasidi's house.

"Have you forgotten that I need you to help me around the house?" asked Rabi. "Why travel all the way to Karkasara and back? You could just leave for school two days early, and stop there on the way."

"I'll need those days to do my shopping for school, that's why I'd rather go today. And what about Bilkisu? Today is Saturday; can't she help you with the chores?"

"Fine, go along then. I may as well get used to it; you'll be back at school soon, and I'll have to manage on my own."

"When the next holidays come, I'll be finished with school. Then it'll be Bilki's turn to go off to boarding school, and I'll be here with you all the time."

"Are you mad?" asked the mother. "Are you going to stay and help me in the kitchen for the rest of your life? Aren't you planning on getting married and moving away? Oh Saudatu, do think of that."

"Yes Baba, but for that to happen I need a boyfriend first! One of the boys I was friendly with has already got married, and the other one can't keep me because he's unemployed."

"Well, maybe you'll meet someone today, on the way to Tasidi's house."

"What a funny thing to say, Baba. It would be shameful to stop and talk to strange young men in the street."

"But that's the best place to meet one. And once you get to talking, all you need to do is tell him where your house is and walk away. He'll come find you if he's interested."

"I prefer to be asked where I come from, Baba. And I don't trust men who like to give girls lifts in their cars."

"You're right, you should be wary of the ones that want to give you a ride—they're all bastards. They just enjoy corrupting girls. Take a taxi, or walk, but never get into someone's car alone."

"By Allah's grace, I'll never be guilty of such behaviour."

"Good. I worry so much about your future... and then I have Bilki to worry about, too, after you. May Allah lead you to your future husband. Oh, but I hope the one He leads you to won't expect me to buy a bunch of things I can't afford."

"Don't say that, Baba. Allah is the source of all our blessings."

"It's too true, Saudatu. Look what happened to me. It's been twenty-one days since I left your father and he hasn't sent us even a single naira. Do you suppose he'll spend anything for your marriage?"

"Forget about him, Baba. He has Allah to contend with. One day, he'll regret the way he's behaved. May you live long!"

This was how Saudatu spoke to her mother, always trying to bring her spirits up. She did everything she could to help her, so that she could have a chance to rest, for Rabi often found herself driven to her wits' end—for example, when school got out and droves of schoolchildren descended on her to buy food. As for Bilkisu, she did the dishes, but not much else; Jamilu did the sweeping; Mustapha and Sani stood at the front door, and took orders from adult male customers who couldn't come inside the house because it would mean breaking purdah. Meanwhile, Rabi's youngest children, Habibu and Hanne, would go on playing mischievous games around the house. Her eldest, Kabiru, was trying to get a job teaching at Jarkasa Primary School. Every morning after breakfast, Rabi would give him one naira for the day. She was also still helping him out with things like bathing soap and detergent for his laundry.

Rabi gave Saudatu two naira for taxi fare as the girl got ready to visit Tasidi, and warned her again not to accept any offers of rides from strange men. Saudatu was dressed beautifully with a big veil and a handbag slung over her shoulder. Though Rabi was the lighter skinned of the two of them, Saudatu was far more beautiful than her mother. She had it all: a long neck, a lovely face and nose, large eyes—and you could tell from one look that given a chance to fill out, she would have a shapely, statuesque figure.

She stood near some date trees on the roadside. Three taxis stopped for her, but when she said she was going to Karkasara, they drove on ahead. One bus driver after another kept stopping for her, and she kept snubbing them, until she began to get quite tired of it.

Then an Alhaji drove by in a flashy gold-coloured car. They locked eyes for a moment, but she looked away, and he passed her without slowing down. She saw him looking back at her, though, as he drove away.

Finally another empty taxi turned up. The driver asked for one naira. She got in and handed him the money. Near Rimi Market, she caught sight of the same Alhaji that had passed her earlier, but he drove on without seeing her.

She reached Tasidi's house at dusk.

Tasidi asked her, "Have you still not found a husband, Saudatu? What are you waiting for? You had better get one before you finish school."

"You know what my boyfriend's like; I can't marry him."

"You mean Gambo, Salamatu's son?"

"Yes, him. I can't aim that low."

"You're right, he's not a good match for you. Usaini asked me about your marriage but only once. I don't know whether I should mention it to him."

"Which Usaini?"

"You know who I'm talking about. What about him? He's been to school, and unlike Gambo, he'll start working soon."

"But by Allah, I don't love him. Besides, I'm taller than he his!"

"So he takes after his mother. Does he have any flaws other than that?"

"No, but... I just don't like him. If he asks you about me again, tell him I've found someone else to marry."

"I will not lie. If you don't like him, we'll leave it at that. Nobody should get married under compulsion."

"Thank you. That's what I wanted to hear. I discussed all this with mother before I came here."

"May Allah let you meet the best man possible. May we marry you off without any regrets."

Tasidi gave Saudatu four bars of soap and a bottle of pomade, while the other women of the house as well as Alhaji Sule gave her gifts of money.

On her way home, Saudatu peered into every gold car that went by, hoping to catch a glimpse of the Alhaji she had seen earlier, but she didn't see him. She hadn't noticed the make of car; all she knew was that it looked expensive and well-maintained.

Over the next week, she made preparations to return to school, but didn't bother to buy too many things. On the day she left, Kabiru came home with the news that his appointment had been confirmed. Up until then, he had been working on a temporary basis, but now he would be earning a proper monthly salary. There was happiness in thát news—but there was still the unhappiness of their mother's divorce. For Saudatu, the subject was so painful that she didn't divulge the secret even to her closest school friends.

Anyway, she thought, school would only last a few more months, and then it would be over. She prayed often to Allah to help her find a husband as soon as she finished school, so that her mother would have the relief of having one less mouth to feed. But she only found time to mull over such worries at bedtime, as most of her day was taken up with schoolwork.

Back at home, Rabi continued her food-selling business, while Kabiru kept at his teaching job. He handed his first monthly salary over to Rabi, keeping just enough for himself to buy three sets of clothes. His mother tried to sound him out about his interest in getting married. Then, after he had eaten supper, she broached the subject of his father. "Do you ever call on Alhaji? If you have, you haven't told me about it."

At this, Kabiru became agitated and very angry. His eyes filled with tears and went bloodshot. After he had wiped his tears, he said to her, "I once went to the house to collect my books, but he wasn't there. I waited for him outside and when he found me there, he said..." Kabiru burst into tears again before he could complete the sentence.

Rabi, who had no tears left to cry anymore, remained in control. She had to let Kabiru cry out whatever pain was in his heart. He was still a boy, after all. He wouldn't be like this once he grew up. Of the two months since they moved from Alhaji Abdu's house, Rabi had spent the first consumed by grief and heartache. She had talked to herself sometimes, absentmindedly, and at night she stayed awake brooding deeply over what had happened.

Her people had upbraided her for keening over her divorce, saying that even if it killed her, Alhaji Abdu probably wouldn't even notice; the loss would only be felt by her children. After some time, she began to heed their advice, giving up thoughts of her former husband and concentrating on her food-selling business and looking after the kids. Her children came first, and whenever any of them had a problem, she would put everything else aside until it was solved. And right now, she was most concerned about Kabiru continuing his education.

Once Kabiru was done crying, he went on. "As soon as he came back, he lambasted me for coming to his house. 'Didn't I tell you all never to come back here?' he shouted. When I told him my reason for coming, he went inside and came back out with the books. He threw them at me and warned me again not to return."

"Why shouldn't you go there? You have every right. It's your father's house. Just let him cool down for a while, and then you can visit again." She hid her real feelings from her son; her heart was boiling with anger.

"Mother, I will never go back to that house. Not even if I'm reduced to such poverty that I have to walk around naked."

"But you will have to talk to your father, especially when the issue of your marriage comes up."

"What marriage, Baba?" Kabiru asked. "I don't think I will marry for another ten years, at least."

"Ten years?" she was flabbergasted. "What are you, a heathen? I've been thinking that after Saudatu gets married, you'll be next."

"First of all, I've only recently begun to work. It'll take two years before I save enough money to see me through college. Then I have to spend four years at the university and another year in the national service. That's seven. After that, it'll probably take me another two years to get settled in a job, and then another year to save enough money to think of getting married. That's ten years, altogether."

"But you'll be an old man by then."

"Baba, you already have to feed and clothe me. If I get married now, you'll have to feed and clothe my wife as well. Don't you think it would be a bit too much for you?

That made Rabi pause. He was right. If he were to think about getting married now, she would have to bear the cost of it. She breathed a sigh of thanks that none of her children had turned out wild or irresponsible; all of them had always been thoughtful and well-behaved.

"How much are the fees for the university?" she asked.

"It doesn't cost anything. In fact, they even give you some allowance to buy books."

"Then why don't you join now? Why go on working for only a hundred and seventy naira a month?"

"Because we need the money right now, that's why."

"I can support you if I have to, Kabiru. Remember that money we deposited in the bank? You can draw from that while you're attending university. As for me, I can take care of your brothers and sisters from the profits of my food trade."

Kabiru was astounded to hear her use his name. He was her first-born, and mothers were not supposed to be so bold as to refer to their first-born children by name.

"The time for feeling bashful and timid are over," she said, when she detected the surprise on his face. "May Allah guide you through your education. How will you go about getting admitted?"

"They've just now started selling the application form. I need to buy one and fill it out."

"How much is it?"

"About ten naira. But Baba, I need to find someone who can help me secure admission—so many people apply to get in, it's very competitive."

"Don't worry. Just buy the form, fill it out, and leave everything else to Allah."

Allahu Akbar! Kabiru went to Bayero University the following day in an ebullient mood and bought the form. And it was his good fortune that he was soon admitted into the engineering program. Rabi gave him whatever money he needed for small purchases while he lived on campus. Neither Rabi nor Kabiru informed Alhaji Abdu of these new developments, afraid that if he knew, he would only cause them more fear and anguish.

‖‖‖

CHAPTER FIVE

‖‖‖

Alhaji Abdu was indeed very enamoured with his new bride. Everything changed after Rabi left the house. He bought chickens every day, or tripe of lamb; and when Delu tired of these, he would switch to fish or ram's head. They never ran out of meat to fry. Besides that, he gave her money for cigarettes, and saw to it that they never ran out of the very expensive kola-nuts.

Delu had him buy a fridge for her so she could sell ice and *kunun-zaki* soft drinks instead of sitting idle all day. Aside from Ladidi, the two of them were mostly alone. No one ever turned up at the house except a few of Delu's unmarried women friends. None of Alhaji Abdu's relations bothered to call on him anymore. It never troubled him. He was concerned with Delu's happiness and no one else's, and would buy her anything she asked for, no matter how hard it was to obtain. He was nearly always at home. He wouldn't go to his fabric stall until eleven o'clock, and even then he would come home for the noon Zuhr prayer. He would leave for work again after lunch, return home at six, and remain indoors until the following morning. Sometimes he and Delu brazenly went to bed together in the daytime, leaving Ladidi in the family compound to keep watch in case any visitors came.

The girl now led a solitary life in Rabi's former room. It took her a while before she got used to it; at first, she was frightened to sleep there alone. As consolation, she had plenty of delicious food to eat, much better fare than she'd had before—but with Delu constantly insulting her and forcing her to do work, she wasn't able to enjoy it very much. Though Ladidi was too afraid to say it to her father, she would have much preferred to call Rabi her mother, and go live with her.

One day, Delu said to her husband on a sudden whim, "Oh, *mai gidan na*, my man-of-the-house... I do so like those gold chokers, with the matching earrings, that have come into fashion. I'd love to have a set."

"How much are they, Delu?" he asked her. "No need to beg for it. I'll buy you anything you want."

That encouraged her to inflate the price. She told him they would cost two hundred and fifty naira instead of two hundred. He handed over the money, and after buying the chain and earrings, she pocketed the balance.

Before very long Delu had filled out so much that she could be heard huffing and puffing as she moved about. Her skin acquired a reddish glow as well. Whenever she went out of the house for any reason, her husband would drive her to her destination and bring her back. But just four months after she married him, she began to feel the itch to go out alone.

One day, Talatu, one of her friends, visited her at home while Alhaji Abdu was away at his stall. They talked about old times, when they had led the loose life together in the red-light district. The house was filled with shouts and ululations, as though they were at an all-female wedding ceremony.

"Oh, I'm sorry," said Talatu after they had laughed together for some time. "I forgot to tell you the message I was sent to give you."

"By who?"

"Who else would send me to give you a message but your favourite friend in the world?"

"You don't mean Alhaji Karanta, do you?"

"Of course I mean him! He's been pestering me for a month to tell you that if you won't end your marriage, then at the very least you ought to come and see him."

"Isn't he bored of me?"

"How can I know, Delu?" asked Talatu. "Perhaps only death can end your love for each other."

"Tell him I won't come. Besides, isn't he married to four wives as it is?"

"You'd be surprised, though. He still sounds very enamoured with you. Do you know he gave me twenty naira just to come and relay his message?"

"Ask him how much he can afford to spend on me."

"He expected you to say that. And he promised to give you whatever you ask for. Just let me know, I'll get it from him and bring it to you myself."

"Tell him I want an atamfa cloth, and enough money to cover the sewing charges. Nothing less."

Talatu returned the following day with what Delu had asked for—and a bottle of perfume thrown in.

Delu lied to her husband, saying that a friend of hers had given birth. The foolish man gave her twenty naira to present as a naming ceremony gift, and without ever suspecting anything, he dropped her off at Talatu's house, where he promised to collect her at half-past-five.

Delu and Talatu flagged a taxi and went directly to Alhaji Karanta's guest house. Talatu left the two of them and returned home. Delu stayed shacked up with Alhaji Karanta from eleven until half-past-four. Then she went back to Talatu's house. She returned with a carrier bag containing the articles her lover had given her: another atamfa cloth, perfume, soap, and the tidy sum of fifty naira. From this she gave Talatu ten naira and two bars of soap for her troubles.

Alhaji Abdu arrived punctually at half-past-five to pick Delu up, imagining that it was a wife he was taking home, when in fact it was a worthless nothing.

||||||

CHAPTER SIX

||||||

A lhaji Abubakar was a businessman born and raised in Kano city. He owned three stalls where he sold imported clothes. He was the only son of his father, Alhaji Barau, and had taken the business over from him. The old man hadn't let his son go beyond secondary school in his education; instead, he had taken him along to the marketplace and taught him to run his business.

Alhaji Barau had married three wives, and had been anxious to sire children. His wives—two of them Nigerian, and the third Nigerien (from the Niger Republic)—all shared his wish, each of them desperately hoping to become pregnant and bear him a child. They beseeched Allah, and did everything they could, but it seemed to be of no use. All their friends and relations came to know about this problem.

Finally, when Alhaji Barau was on the verge of resigning himself to a childless old age, Allah heard his prayers, and Fatima, his Nigerien wife, became pregnant. She didn't divulge the news to anyone until after the first trimester, out of fear that the jealousy of the other wives might bring about an unlucky end the pregnancy. Finally, in her fourth month, when it was her turn to cook for the family, she went to Alhaji Barau's room and informed him of her condition. He laughed, he cheered, he even wept, so overcome was he with joy. Seeing him cry as he thanked Allah for blessing him, Fatima burst into tears, too. He stayed awake the whole night, unable to sleep a wink. Fatima told him that she was terrified to have the baby in Nigeria; she begged him to let her return to her country and give birth to the baby there. She told him how dangerous it would be to let out the news, as jealous people might go to any lengths to end the pregnancy.

Alhaji Barau thought it over. He supposed it was a good idea to keep things secret for a little while, but he couldn't imagine even his worst enemy ever trying to harm Fatima. He decided he would pray to Allah to protect Fatima and her baby—but he wouldn't dream of allowing her to travel across the border to her home town of Maradi in Niger. She would remain in his house and deliver the child there. He cautioned her not to let anybody know about her pregnancy for the next one week, during which time he would ask his mullahs to pray for them.

Even though they were kept in the dark, the other two wives noticed the changes in Fatima's and Alhaji Barau's behaviour. Fatima started receiving a special concoction every day that had been poured over Qur'anic slates and was kept in an earthenware pot in her room. She drank no other liquid. Marabouts began to visit, many of them, to serve her the drink and to work other charms to deter anyone bent on harming the woman.

The other two wives grew more and more curious until one of them, the senior wife, finally discovered what was going on. She waited until Alhaji Barau called Fatima to his room for a talk and then secretly followed her. She knew that he had begun calling Fatima to his room three times a day—in the morning, in the afternoon, and again as soon as he returned from the market at night. This time, the senior wife eavesdropped on their conversation, and heard him ask Fatima to be sure to drink up the concoction and not to miss the prescribed timings. She instantly became jealous and angry when she realized that her suspicions about the pregnancy were true after all.

Fatima had for some time now been wearing a veil draped over her face, even inside the house. She came out, salaamed, and went into the kitchen, as it was her turn to cook for the family that day.

The senior wife didn't waste any time. She immediately burst in and asked her husband the reason for all the secrecy. She could be counted among those who would congratulate him on the happy occasion, she told him, but he shouldn't hold it against them for not conceiving first.

Alhaji Barau became very angry and he turned swiftly on her, lambasting her for eavesdropping until she rushed out of the room in tears. She swore then that she would put an end to the pregnancy even if it meant pawning every last thing she owned. And true to this oath, she paid enormous sums of money to marabouts to see that Fatima miscarried—but to no avail. Each one of them, after collecting his fee and attempting to work some magic, had told her that it was impossible. It could not be done, they said, and she had better give up. After many failures, she decided to change tactics. Rather than end the pregnancy, she would have the marabouts try to cause Fatima to become mentally deranged, or to contract some incurable disease before she carried the baby to term. And soon after she began this new effort, the first wife got what she wanted.

It happened one day at half-past-one. Her husband had come home to perform his ritual ablutions before he went to the Friday congregational prayer when Fatima suddenly rushed out of her room in a frenzy, shouting and yelling unintelligibly. The house-helps immediately caught hold of her, but she tried to wrest herself from their grasp. Her husband was called in to see her deranged condition for himself. With a loud shriek, she broke free of the three women holding her, throwing all of them to the ground—and then collapsed herself and began writhing on the floor. Alhaji Barau sent for more help. It took five men to hold her still and prevent her from falling again and harming the foetus.

After the prayer was over, mullahs were called in, and dispersed to pray in different parts of the house. One of Fatima's sisters, who had come to Kano along with her from Niger, sat with her in her room. Meanwhile, the senior wife, despite all the commotion, stayed in her own room and didn't come out until well after four o'clock. When she finally did come out, she lied that she had been asleep all along. She didn't seem bothered in the slightest about having done nothing while women from the neighbourhood who lived several houses away had rushed over to help. Even the second wife, whose turn it was to cook that day, had lent a helping hand.

A day later, Fatima's condition took a turn for the better. She began to talk quickly in Zabarma, so that only her sister could make any sense of what she was saying. Then, in the flicker of an eye, her sister got up, adjusted her wrap and tied it again so it was tight and secure around her waist, and marched out of the room. A moment later, everyone heard the senior wife screaming for help from inside her room. They rushed in to find Fatima's sister straddling her and punching her. They were trying desperately to pull her away when Alhaji Barau, who was sitting outside with the mullahs, rushed in to see what was going on. He pulled Fatima's sister away and demanded an explanation. She refused to give him any, and asked him instead to send for the Nigerien wife of a friend of his, at whose wedding he had met and proposed to Fatima.

The woman lived nearby, and her husband happened to call on Alhaji Barau just then to express his sympathies regarding Fatima's illness. Alhaji Barau begged him to send his wife over to translate what Fatima was saying. Once she arrived, Alhaji Barau invited her and all the people around to go in as witnesses to hear what she had to say.

The translator said that Fatima was begging for the senior wife to rid her of the evil spell that had been placed on her. She said she felt as though her flesh was being consumed, and she was slowly losing her sight.

Moving swiftly, Alhaji Barau went and dragged his senior wife out of her room, and began beating her right there in front of the whole gathered crowd. He wasn't known as a wife-beater, but this time he made her suffer. Afterwards he sent for her family and demanded that they force her to lift the spell she had cast on Fatima before nightfall. They succeeded in getting her to tell the name of the marabout she had gotten to work the magic. They also learned that the *sammu* fetish which held the power of the spell had been hidden in a hollow of a baobab tree.

Alhaji Barau sent for the marabout, who came and revealed the location of the tree. He was escorted to the place and returned with the *sammu*. He opened the package and picked out the contents, which included a lock of Fatima's hair. A special powder had also been blown around Fatima's room, though, and that was not so easy to get rid of. On the instructions of the marabout, she moved out of her room and moved into Alhaji Barau's sitting room.

He gave the marabout a good deal of money and implored him to do whatever he could to ensure that Fatima was restored to health, promising even more money if he succeeded. The marabout left after reassuring Alhaji Barau that he would get down to it without delay. Yet it was nearly a fortnight before Fatima was back in full health.

After not too much longer, she went into labour and gave birth to a boy. Both she and her husband were overjoyed and very grateful to Allah. On the third day after the birth, Alhaji Barau handed the first wife a letter announcing his divorce three times, meaning that it was over between the two of them for good. He warned her that if anything turned out amiss concerning his wife or child, he would bring her before a court of law. The marabout had warned him that a complete recovery might take some time, and even then he couldn't rule out the possibility that the nursing mother might suffer a relapse and begin behaving abnormally.

For Alhaji Barau and Fatima, the child they named Abubakar was like the lone piece of meat in a pot of soup. They watched over him carefully, making sure that nothing untoward happened to him. Thus he grew up with his every whim indulged, as if he were a prince. Still, his parents raised him to show respect to people and to have good manners. They taught him to understand that relationships between people transcend the value of money, and that there is a limit to what money can get out of a man.

Abubakar's education stopped after the secondary level, when his father began showing him the ropes at the marketplace. When he was old enough to marry, a match was found for him, the beautiful daughter of a business-man. Five years later, he took a second wife. Unlike his father, he had no difficulties in producing offspring, and soon had four children—three borne by the first wife, and one by the second.

Yet theirs wasn't a happy family. The wives quarrelled nearly every day, and held their husband in contempt, saying he was too meek.

CHAPTER SEVEN

||||||

A lhaji Abubakar's posh house was situated in the centre of Kano, at the end of a long drive which meandered from the gate until it linked up with a bigger, newly widened road. Large neem trees stood outside. The guest wing was close to his well-appointed sitting room, while the family wing was deep inside the building. Each wife had two lavishly furnished rooms, an inner bedroom and a parlour, as well as a kitchen, a store closet, and a bathroom. The house was filled with electronic gadgets, including an intercom that connected the wives' rooms with those of their husband.

In Alhaji Abubakar's service were two night-watchmen, a house-help, a cook, and a laundryman. He also employed another house-help for each of his wives. His senior wife, Hajiya Amina, had three children, and the second, Hajiya Halima, only one child. These two women could not go three days at a stretch without getting into a fight. Hajiya Amina was quick to retaliate to even the slightest perceived snub. As for Hajiya Halima, she lacked manners and looked down on everyone, including her husband. She had finished secondary school before she married Alhaji Abubakar. Hajiya Amina had attended a mixed Western and Islamiyya School. Her marriage to Abubakar had been tempestuous, despite the fact that he was patient and accommodating, and only ever protested as a last resort.

Alhaji Abubakar had once had a misunderstanding with Hajiya Amina that had led to her running back to her parents' home in a spiteful rage. He had finally taken exception to the impatience and high-handed manner with which she treated his domestic staff, but when he tried to bring her to order, she had given him a dressing down in front of everyone. He had become so angry that the house-helps had to lead him outside to save his wife from a severe beating. That was when she had run away to her parents. When Alhaji Abubakar asked her to come back to his house, her parents dragged their feet for some time, until at last he had taken the opportunity of her absence to marry Hajiya Halima.

Hajiya Amina stayed away for four months at her parents' house, where her mother had her own husband completely under her thumb. She prevented him from having any say in his daughter's marital problems until the day they heard that Alhaji Abubakar was about to take a second wife. She tried paying the local marabouts to see that the marriage came to naught, but their efforts were futile. When the new bride joined her daughter's husband, Hajiya Amina's mother had no other option but to take her back to her husband's house. At that time, Hajiya Amina was expecting her second child.

After taking up residence again, Hajiya Amina tried to treat her husband the same way her mother had treated hers. Her failure led to frequent skirmishes in the house after Hajiya Halima joined the family. Hajiya Halima, too, came from an affluent family—perhaps even a bit more affluent than her co-wife's. Thus each of them in her own way tried to wield as much power as she could around the house.

Amidst all this it was Alhaji Abubakar who suffered the most. He became utterly fed up with his life on account of the poor relations between the two women. The only time anyone ever saw him smiling was when he was outside his house, either when he was in one of his stalls or at a friend's house. His friends were aware of his situation and sympathized with him, advising him to be patient and to hope for things to change. And so life went on until he had the idea of taking a third wife, who might bring the first two wives to their senses.

He spent the next three months trying to make a choice, but none of the girls he met seemed satisfactory. He felt he would need only a single look into her eyes to know if a girl was right for him, whether he saw her on the road or among a group of customers.

Finally, he did see one—but that one quick look into her eyes was all he got, at first.

It happened to be on a day when trouble was brewing in his house, this time over the cooking of food. The senior wife had asked the cook to make rice and stew for her and her children, but Hajiya Halima, whose turn it was to share her husband's bed and supervise the cooking, asked for stew for herself, her husband, and the staff. The cook informed Hajiya Halima that there wasn't enough stew to go around, and that it was getting too late to cook more. She asked him angrily to cook a simple yam pottage instead for the whole family. She wasn't bothered whether the food would be to everyone's liking. The cook, who usually tried to find ways to do as little work as possible, quickly cooked up the yam and served it. Hajiya Amina descended on him and demanded to know why he had failed to do as she'd asked.

"I'm sorry, Hajiya," said the cook. "Because the stew wouldn't go around, Hajiya Halima asked me to cook yam pottage."

"Why didn't you come and tell me that before? Go take this food to her and ask her to send it to her family."

"Please understand, Hajiya. It was already getting dark—"

"Get out of my sight!"

He took the food away. Neither he nor Hajiya Amina knew that Hajiya Halima had eavesdropped on their conversation. She went and stood at the entrance of her co-wife's sitting room, with her arms akimbo.

"Listen, my parents don't depend on this house for their meals. It's your relatives who are the poor and needy ones."

"Who are you calling poor?" asked Hajiya Amina. "Remember, you worthless slut, that your parents didn't even give you a *gara* when you got married. It was only after you gave birth to your first child that they got you one."

"Well it's a sure thing that your father couldn't have bought one for me. Come out, if you dare, so I can give you a good thrashing!"

"What is the matter?" asked their husband. "There is never any peace in this house! What's going on?"

Hajiya Halima told him everything, claiming that she wasn't at fault, because it was her turn to cook.

"Don't you feel ashamed, fighting like this every day? What is wrong with you?"

"You always side with her," said Hajiya Amina. "Why should she ask the cook to cook something different from what I asked him?"

"You're despicable," said Hajiya Halima. "It's my turn to oversee the cooking. Why can't you wait your turn and then do what you like? You think you can just throw your weight around however you want."

"I learned that from your mother."

"No, I think you mean you learned it from your own mother. I've seen the way your father has to ask her for permission every time he wants to piss."

"So it seems I'm powerless to get you two to quiet down," said their husband. "Look, I've had it. Both of you get out of my house immediately—and don't think you can leave with any of my children. You crude, worthless women! Do you think I can't marry again, if and when I want?"

The domestic staff gathered around and tried to persuade him to change his mind. They had never before heard him even raise his voice towards his wives, much less send them away. Everyone was astonished at his adamancy. In the end, though, he relented, and went upstairs to his room.

In the morning, he ignored Hajiya Halima when she knocked on his door to serve him tea (which was the only thing his wives ever prepared for him themselves; all the other cooking was done by the help). He didn't come out until eleven o'clock, and when he did, he left for his stall without talking to anybody or handing over the money for the day's purchases. He drove off in a huff, and was brooding over his latest domestic crisis when a bus driver stopped suddenly in front of him. While swerving to avoid the bus, he looked to the side... and locked eyes with a girl who was standing on the curb with a bag slung over her shoulder.

He fell for her instantly.

But he couldn't stop. There were cars close behind him. He drove ahead but kept looking back until he reached the junction near Murtala Hospital, when he decided to turn around. He drove back in a hurry, but found that the girl was no longer there. He waited there for some time, thinking of her and trying to conjure up the image of her face. There was nothing else he could do.

He had simply fallen in love with her. It wasn't even on account of her beauty—it was just the look in her eyes.

He drove on to his stall and spent the whole day in deep thought, not speaking to anyone, and returned home at eleven o'clock that night. It wasn't usual for him to come home so late; he was generally always back by sundown. Once he reached the house, he parked his car in the garage and went straight upstairs, avoiding his family, and lay down on his bed.

This went on for three days, and his wives began to get very worried about it. But they didn't bring it up with him.

On the following day, he called them both to his room and cautioned them about their behaviour. "I asked you to leave, but you stayed put," he said. "Now listen: By Allah, if either one of you goes back to your old ways, I'll divorce you. Neither one of you is compelled to stay in this house."

The women's faces registered the shock they felt at his words. He had taken them by surprise, and for some time afterwards, it seemed to have an effect. But a person's nature is like something engraved in stone; and before too long, both of them lapsed back into the petty arguments he had warned them to avoid.

Meanwhile, Alhaji Abubakar prayed fervently every day for another glimpse of the girl. Finally, after three months, he got one. The girl, of course, was Rabi's daughter Saudatu. It had taken her three months to finish her secondary school studies, and now she had returned home for good.

It so happened that Alhaji Abubakar was out driving with a friend of his named Alhaji Uba when he saw her standing at the same place he had seen her before; only this time she was with an older woman, waiting for a taxi. He slammed on the brakes hard enough to give his friend a bit of a scare. He parked very close to the women, got out of the car, and addressed them. "Hello. How do you do?"

"Fine," Rabi answered. "How do you do, Alhaji?"

Her daughter, who recognised him and realized that his eyes kept moving over to her, bowed her head and let them exchange greetings.

"Where are you going?"

"We want to go to Karkasara," said Rabi. "We're waiting for a taxi."

"You'll get tired waiting for one. Let me give you a lift. It will be quicker."

Alhaji Abubakar was overjoyed to have met Saudatu again after three months of thinking about her. He adjusted his rear-view mirror so he could see her face and kept stealing looks at her as he drove. Once they had arrived at their destination, he asked them when they planned to return. Rabi explained that they wouldn't be going back before the Zuhr noontime prayer. With that, she quickly went indoors.

Before Saudatu could follow her in, he stopped her. "Excuse me, but what's the hurry? What is your name?"

"Saudatu."

"Which school do you go to?"

"I went to Dala. I just wrote my final exams this week."

"Thank God. I hope you are not married?"

"If I were a married woman, I wouldn't have spoken to you."

"I suppose that's true. But do you have any boyfriends?"

"I have several."

"If I show interest in you... will I have any hope?"

"Of course."

"Good! That's what I wanted to hear! I'll come back later and drive you home. I want to know where you live."

"I'll see you then."

Alhaji Abubakar had already told his friend Alhaji Uba about Saudatu, and about the day he had seen her there waiting for a taxi. On his way to drop his friend off, he also told him about the problems he was having with his wives. After the noontime prayer, he came back to the house and sent a boy in to inform Saudatu of his arrival. Back at home, he parked the car on the street and followed the women into the narrow alley leading to the house. Rabi hastened ahead of them, while the other two walked with moderate steps.

Alhaji Abubakar told Saudatu that he would visit her at nightfall. He left after giving her a fifty naira gift.

She remained standing in deep thought in the entranceway. She was somewhat taken aback by this turn of events. She had never possessed so much money before in her life. On a sudden whim, she stole a quick look at the departing Alhaji, only to catch his eyes: he had turned to look back at her too. They waved at each other, happily.

CHAPTER EIGHT

A little after eight o'clock that night, Alhaji Abubakar said his Isha' prayers and had a bath. He dressed in a hurry and sprayed a pleasant perfume all over his expensive clothes. Like a boy falling in love for the first time, he was anxious to go and meet Saudatu again. It seemed like ages since they had last parted, and he thought the time would never come. As far as he was concerned the wedding could take place in two weeks, provided she was agreeable to the idea. To be sure, he hadn't yet talked to her long enough to know her very well, but he didn't believe she would spurn his advances. Though now, suddenly, that possibility began to worry him. If she turned him down, how very long it would take before would be able to forget her!

Still worrying, he was on his way out when Hajiya Amina, following him, said, "I told you I had somewhere I had to go, and you promised to take me. But now I see that you're leaving on your own."

"Yes, I'm going out somewhere," he said. "Don't worry; I'll take you tomorrow."

"Oh, Alhaji, but you promised—and here I am ready to go," Hajiya Amina protested.

"I said we'll go tomorrow. Do you *have* to go today?"

"I must. I can go by taxi."

"You want to hire a taxi just to go out visiting? The way you act sometimes! I forbid it! Though I suppose you'll do as you like, regardless."

He heard her say, as he turned to go, "If it were Hajiya Halima, you would have consented to it. But me, I'm worthless as far as you are concerned."

"You heard what I said."

"I can pay my own way, you know."

He left, ignoring her. He drove to Saudatu's house, thinking of nothing but her the whole way. He parked his car at Shahuci Primary School and walked with a swagger up to the house. After a brief wait, he sent a boy in to announce his arrival. People passed up and down the alley as he waited. Presently, Saudatu came out holding a mat, which she spread on the ground for them. Then she knelt and greeted him.

"Welcome."

"Hello, Saudatu. How are you?"

"I'm fine. How was the trip back home?"

"It was fine... but I couldn't eat anything. I was too busy thinking of you."

She tilted her head down and smiled, thinking. He hadn't been able to eat, he said—well, as for her, she had been practically incapacitated the whole day. Every time she thought of him, or he was mentioned in conversation, she felt a thrill run down her spine. She thought of Tasidi's reaction after Rabi had told her how Alhaji Abubakar had greeted them. Tasidi had beseeched Allah to listen to her own prayers as closely as He listened to Saudatu's. This man was so rich, Tasidi said, that Rabi and her daughter would surely be better off for it.

Rabi, on the other hand, hadn't been so sure. She reminded Tasidi that his wives wouldn't sit idle if they heard that he was taking a third wife. They would certainly seek the help of local marabouts to do something about it. The wives of the rich always hated it when their husbands married other women. Rabi was also worried about how she would afford the marriage gifts she'd be expected to send along with her daughter to the house of a rich husband. But Tasidi asked her not to despair. She had advised Saudatu to be on her best behaviour whenever Alhaji Abubakar called, and never to contradict him.

His voice interrupted Saudatu's thoughts. "What is your idea of the kind of man you want to marry?"

"I don't understand," she answered.

"I mean, would you prefer a civil servant or a businessman? An educated man? A member of a royal family?"

She thought carefully before speaking. "It is for Allah to choose, and I will accept whoever He chooses for me."

Surprised by her answer, but also relieved, he went on to say, "But do you prefer an unmarried youth or a married man? I don't mean an *old* man, though. Which one do you prefer?"

"Only Allah knows the unknown. I can't know which among all these different sorts of men is fated to marry me. So how can I tell you?"

Alhaji Abubakar felt it was now time to tell her something about himself, what he did for a living, and the size of his family. She didn't interrupt him or ask any questions until he had finished.

"So what do you think, Saudatu?" he asked after telling her everything about himself. "Do you love me? Will you marry me?"

She didn't know how to answer a question she felt was couched in an appeal. Refusing to answer him, she said, "You have told almost everything I wanted to know, but you left out one very important detail."

He went over in his mind all that he had told her, but couldn't think of anything he'd left out. He wondered whether this was just her way of telling him that she didn't love him. It was terribly frustrating; she wasn't even looking at him, just staring at the floor. "Saudatu," he demanded, "what have I left out that's still keeping you from saying whether or not you love me? You don't love me, do you? Should I give up on you, Saudatu?"

"It isn't a question of whether I love you or not. It's just that... well, you've called me by name several times... but I still don't know yours."

"So that's it! I haven't told you my name!" he cried. "I'm sorry. My name is Alhaji Abubakar Barau. Do you like it?"

"It's very important-sounding."

"Is that so? Well then, let's continue from where we left off! Do you love me? Will you marry me?"

"Suppose that I didn't. It wouldn't be proper to say so directly to your face."

"This is no time for worrying about what's proper. I want you to come out and tell me plainly. When it comes to the question of marriage, you shouldn't hold back your feelings."

"All right then... I love you. I want to marry you and live with you till the end of our days."

"You'll be patient with me, and not get exasperated with my character?"

"As the eloquent among our people say, admiration makes one blind to flaws. I can put up with anything, provided you look out for my welfare."

"Thank God, that is what I hoped to hear. As long as you abide by my wishes and do what I ask of you, we will live in peace forever. And I will do whatever you ask of me."

"So be it."

"But there is one thing."

"What is it?"

"You said someone else had proposed to you. Since you've said you will marry me, you must now forget about anyone else. I will start making preparations for our marriage tomorrow. What do you say?"

"No problem. But let it begin after you have brought the marriage gifts."

"All right. I hope that you will return any gifts that were brought to you by others."

Looking at his watch, he was astonished to see that it was a quarter to midnight. He was overjoyed with how things had turned out, and relieved that she had accepted his proposal. Now the rest was up to him. He gave her a parting gift of one hundred naira and said to her, "That's for you. Tell your mother that I will send a delegation tomorrow night, after which I'll pay you another visit."

"All right," said Saudatu. "May we see you tomorrow in good health."

"Remember your promise."

"God willing, I will do so."

As he drove home, he went over and over their conversation in his mind. He arrived home at midnight and was surprised to find the door unlocked. He cautioned his guards to be more vigilant, as there had been several robberies in the locality.

One of the guards, perhaps out of a mischievous urge to stir up trouble, said to him: "We had locked that door, earlier, not realizing that your senior wife was still out. We only unlocked it when she came back."

Alhaji Abubakar was surprised to hear that Hajiya Amina hadn't returned until so late in the night, but he didn't say anything to the guard except, "Is she back? Fine then. Good night."

He went to Hajiya Amina's room, where he found her sitting with one leg crossed over the other, having tea and biscuits.

She gave him a sidelong glance, then looked away with an insolent expression on her face.

"Didn't I ask you not to go out?" he asked her.

She ignored him.

"Didn't you hear what I said? Has it really come to this—you're not even speaking to me? It's late now, but I want you to pack and leave my house first thing tomorrow morning. You can go and play the role of a queen somewhere else."

"You should give me my divorce letter first," she said to him, as he turned to go out. "I don't have to live with you."

"That won't be necessary. I'll send the letter to your home."

"All right. Makes no difference to me."

In the morning, she cooked breakfast for him, including tea, Irish potatoes and an omelette, and took it to his room after she had her bath. She heard him in his bedroom getting dressed. She put the tray on the table and sat down to wait for him.

When he came out five minutes later, he ignored her.

Realizing that he wasn't going to talk to her, she said, "I want money to prepare the meals for the day."

Instead, he handed her the divorce letter she had demanded on the previous day, and walked out with his car keys in his hands. He gave Hajiya Halima the money and instructed her to lock his room after Hajiya Amina had come out.

Hajiya Amina took her own time to do so, and when she did, she looked bewildered. After collecting all her children, she left with them in tow, including her house-help.

As for Hajiya Halima, it was a festive day for her, a day full of cheer and laughter. She even told the cook not to bother cooking for everyone, just for himself—she would make food for everyone else.

Her husband went straight to his father's house and found his father and mother counting the business profits from the day before. He greeted them and told them that he had met a girl he wanted to marry. His mother criticized him for wanting to marry so many times.

"What are you trying to do, fill up your house with women? Isn't two wives enough?"

"Let him be," said his father. "After all, he can marry up to four."

"You spoil him," his mother told her husband. "So he does whatever he likes."

"I want you to inform Hajiya Jimmai and the others," said her son, "that I will send a driver to take them to deliver the zance gifts after the Isha' prayer."

"What's the big hurry?" asked his mother.

"The girl has already finished school. I think her family wants to marry her off soon."

"You insist on marrying these educated girls who quarrel incessantly in your house."

"I have divorced Hajiya Amina."

"Did she have another fight with Hajiya Halima?" asked his mother.

Alhaji Abubakar explained to his parents the reasons he had handed her the letter of divorce.

"You overreacted," said his mother. "Why couldn't you have tried to stay calm? It isn't good to divorce a woman with children. Show some sense, and let us go and appeal to her to come back."

"I am tired of her treating me with contempt. I will go and get my children from her."

His father said, "Since he is going to marry again, we shouldn't bother about taking her back."

"Oh Alhaji," said his wife, "what about the children? Will they remain with her?"

"Why should they?" asked her husband. "They can stay here with us, since the other wife already has her own children to look after. As for my son, why should he go on living with a despicable woman who holds him in contempt?"

Alhaji Abubakar went straightaway to the market and spent a wad of money buying articles for the courtship gifts. He was rich, after all. He bought a dozen six-yard lengths of material, a dozen blouses, a dozen sets of undergarments, three pairs of shoes, three handbags, two necklaces, and two wristwatches. In addition to all this he included two hundred naira cash. He had these articles delivered to his parents' house in the late afternoon, with instructions to his mother that they should be conveyed to Saudatu's house by early evening. His parents argued that it was too much, that he should reduce the amount of clothes and accessories he was giving, but he disagreed and held firm.

While her former husband was busy shopping at the market, Hajiya Amina was having her belongings packed. Her husband had written the pronouncement of divorce three times on the one letter, making it final. She left taking her breastfeeding child with her, and sent her two older children to their paternal grandparents, with the promise to send the younger one after weaning him.

Alhaji Abubakar drove a few of his women relatives to Saudatu's house to deliver the wedding gifts. His grandmother teased him, in the Hausa tradition, pretending that he was her husband and she was upset over having a new rival. Alhaji Abubakar didn't respond at first, but eventually her humour got the better of him and he shared in the cheerful banter that filled the car, punctuated by peals of laughter from the other women. Once they arrived, he pointed the house out to them, then went back to the car to wait. He soon became restless; he wanted to take the women back home soon, so he could return on his own and see his beloved again.

||||||||||

CHAPTER NINE

Alhaji Abdu arrived to pick Delu up from her friend's house at four-thirty in the afternoon. When she came out of the house, she was moving unsteadily, as though drunk or groggy from sleep, and he wondered if there was something wrong. When he asked her what was the matter, she said, "My stomach hurts, and I think I have a fever." Then she leaned back lazily on the seat. "I've been waiting for you to come and pick me up. I just want to go home, take some medicine, and go to bed."

"Maybe we should go to a chemist, and get you an injection," said Alhaji Abdu. "Wouldn't that be better? Why do you want to go straight home?"

"You know I hate injections, Alhaji. Just take me home."

"All right. Let's go."

Alhaji Abdu stopped at a chemist anyway, and Delu was forced to get a shot and take some pills. She went home and lay in bed without bothering even to change her clothes or cook for the family, who had to spend the remaining part of the day without anything to eat. At seven o'clock the next morning, she begged him to buy some food for them all, saying she was ravenously hungry. He went to Fagge Quarters and bought enough to go around.

It had been going on like this for some time. Whenever Delu wanted to meet Alhaji Karanta, she would tell her husband some lie to get him to take her to a meeting point. Sometimes she didn't even bother with the lie and just took a taxi instead. Before long she had other lovers, too, including a young electrician whom her husband had engaged to repair an electrical fault in the house. The young man had understood how she felt about him from the looks she kept giving him. Her husband had told him to get on with the job and then left the house, asking Delu to pay him when he was finished. They had slept together, and from that day onwards, he would turn up at the house every three or four days asking if there were any more problems with the electrical wiring. She would jump up quickly the moment she heard his salaam; it was she who needed attention, not the wiring. Of course, these visits always happened when her husband was away from the house.

Delu knew a *boka*, a soothsayer, whom she had contacted to prepare a concoction that she used to keep Alhaji Abdu under her power. She had given her body to the *boka*, too—he had not had to bargain very hard for it. So Delu ended up with three different lovers.

Alhaji Abdu never suspected anything. He still believed his wife was a devout woman, and could not imagine that any of the things people said about her were true, let alone raise any objection to her behaviour himself. It never seemed to bother him that nobody visited the house anymore except Delu's friends. As far as he was concerned, she was all the family he needed.

His heart had hardened against Rabi so much that he never even thought of her, let alone her children. They had now been separated for five months, but he had not sent them a thing. He wasn't bothered about their welfare in the slightest. He didn't care whether they were sick or in good health. The only time he had met any of the children was the day Kabiru had come to collect his books. Then one day while out driving, he saw Bilkisu about to cross the road. She waved at him, but he snubbed her and drove past.

Bilkisu ran like mad until she was back home. Panting, she told Rabi who she had seen. "It was father in his car! I kept waving at him, but he ignored me!"

"He must not have seen you," said Rabi. "Otherwise he wouldn't have failed to wave back."

"By Allah, he saw me. We looked in each other's eyes, and then he just..."

"Keep quiet," Rabi interrupted her. "You talk too much. Pick up a dish and get your food."

Rabi stopped her daughter because she couldn't bear to hear about the hateful incident. The fact that his attitude still hadn't changed worried her. She wondered what she would do now that Saudatu had a suitor who wanted to marry her. Who should she approach? Alhaji Abdu? Or would it be better to ask his brother, Alhaji Bello? She worried that if they went to Alhaji Abdu, he might treat them with such contempt that it would take a long time to get over the insult.

Rabi was thankful that the exchanging of wedding gifts didn't involve any men: it was women's business. The men would be involved later—it was for them to go and announce the acceptance of Alhaji Abubakar's proposal before the marriage was solemnized. Meanwhile, she had sent for Tasidi, and asked her to stay around and be among the women who would receive the gifts. Still, Rabi felt very anxious. Today was the day the wedding of her daughter would be fixed; she prayed to Allah to bless the marriage and see that everything turned out well.

Tasidi turned up at six o'clock that evening, and Rabi said to her, "Tasidi, you've come so early! Why didn't you wait until after the Magrib prayer?"

"Oh, Rabi," said Tasidi, pulling up a chair and sitting near her sister, "you know I wouldn't have been able to get a taxi that late."

"That's true, of course. But what about going back home?"

"Alhaji and I agreed that I could spend the night here if I couldn't find a taxi. Look at us, we haven't even exchanged greetings yet, and here we are talking about taxis! How was your afternoon?"

"Fine. Where is your husband? He dropped in here some time ago—he even gave me some money."

"He's doing well. Have you invited Salamatu?"

"I have, and she promised to come."

Saudatu came in and greeted Tasidi. "Welcome. How is Alhaji?"

"He's fine. So what have you been doing? Sitting alone in your room, I suppose? I can't ask you about your schoolwork, now that your school is over."

"The next place to go is the university."

"What university? Or do you mean the university of your husband's house? Come, tell me about him."

"Oh, Baba, what do you mean 'husband'? I don't have any husband yet!" Saudatu said, smiling.

"Let's go to the room and talk about it," said Tasidi.

Rabi didn't follow them; instead, she picked up a *buta* of water and went to the toilet. She had just finished performing her ablutions and come out when she heard the prayer call from the Friday Mosque. She went in and found Saudatu and Tasidi giggling together. Seeing that they had not heard the call, much less gotten up to pray, she said to them, "You'd better pray first, and then go on with your chat."

"I'm on my period," said Tasidi. "I can't pray for the next three days."

"This girl is too," said Rabi. "It's as if she's your own daughter; she does as you do. As for me, though, I had better go and pray."

Before she had completed her *sallata*, women began to troop into the house. Saudatu and Tasidi were still talking when they heard some women salaam from the courtyard. On a sign from Tasidi, Saudatu rushed into the inner room. The long-awaited visitors would expect her to be modest and bashful, and not to appear before them with the other women.

"Salamu alaikum," said one of the newcomers. "Peace be upon you."

"You are welcome," said Tasidi. "Come right in."

The visitors sat on mats which had been specially spread out for them. After they had exchanged greetings, one of them leaned forward and said, "Our son has seen and fallen in love with your daughter, and she has returned his love. That is why we have brought these gifts, for you to accept, and thus give your blessings to the marriage. Today, we seek to establish a friendly alliance with you."

"If you accept our proposal," added one of Alhaji Abubakar's aunts, "we should pray for Allah's blessings, which all of us yearn for."

Tasidi came forward, placed her hands on the boxes and said, "We accept your proposal and we are very happy about it, because marriage is one of the traditions of the Prophet. We hope we have started on the right foot. May Allah bless us all, amin."

All the women repeated the word amin, and Tasidi went to one of the large chests, which was mounted on wheels so it rolled, and opened it so that the contents could be seen by everyone present. It was filled with cosmetics: there were pomades, perfumes, powder, and lipstick of many varieties. There was also a gold chain and a matching set of earrings, bangles, wristwatches, skirts, bras and panties, two atamfa cloths, and six headscarves. Except for the atamfa and the headscarves, there were twelve of each article, and resting on top of all these things was the sum of two hundred naira.

Tasidi locked up the boxes and said to the visitors, "We are indeed very happy to say we have seen everything. May Allah let us witness this wedding, for He alone allows one to breathe out after breathing in."

"No mistake about that," said an elderly woman visitor. "May Allah bless us all with long lives. Please, get in touch with us soon, as we want the wedding to take place as soon as possible."

"We have no objections," said Tasidi. "God willing, it will happen."

On their way out, the visitors said, "We leave you in peace. May Allah bless the marriage. We look forward to seeing you tomorrow or the day after with the good news."

"Good night, farewell, and thank you all. May Allah see you safely home."

The visitors left in good spirits, and left their hosts in even greater spirits; for the love that brought the man and girl together was reciprocal—which usually meant that it would be long-lasting. The reciprocity of affection on the part of the lovers rubbed off on their families.

Rabi gave copious thanks to Allah for making possible what she had so fervently hoped for, what she had been beseeching Him for, every day of her life for years.

"There is nothing for us to do but express our heartfelt gratitude to Him. Look at the quality of these gifts! Only the daughters of the most elite families receive their wedding gifts in chests on rolling wheels! Thanks be to Allah!" Rabi picked up a kola-nut, broke it into two and handed Tasidi one lobe, saying, "We should take the crate to Alhaji Bello's house in Soron Dinki and tell him about the request the visitors have made concerning the marriage. If he meets Alhaji Abubakar tomorrow, we can go tomorrow evening and hear how the meeting went, and then relay the news the following day."

"All right," said Tasidi. "I suppose we must keep the father's side informed as to what's going on. Who do you think should escort us?"

"Soron Dinki isn't far. Ibrahim can come with us. Let me call him."

Ibrahim and Kabiru came in. "Baba, whose box is that?" Ibrahim asked Rabi.

Tasidi answered him. "Saudatu's."

"Saudatu's? Did Baba buy it for her?"

"You know Rabi couldn't have afforded this. This is Allah's doing."

"Tell me, please! Who gave it to her?"

"You are very stupid," Kabiru told Ibrahim. "They're courtship gifts, aren't they?"

"Yes, they're Saudatu's *zance* gifts, sent by a rich Alhaji," said Rabi.

"Is that whose car I saw yesterday?"

"Yes. He wants a quick marriage."

"Lucky Saudatu!" said Ibrahim.

The two boys escorted Rabi and Tasidi to the house of Alhaji Bello. They were met by Hajiya Hauwa, his wife.

"Welcome, Rabi," she said. "Welcome, Tasidi. Come in and sit down."

"How has the day been?" asked Rabi. "How are the children? How are you all faring?"

"We're all fine. How's your food-selling business? Mine hasn't been good; I always seem to have food left unsold at the end of the day."

"Is that so? But that's business. That's how it was when I started, too."

"It's good to see you in our house, Tasidi," said Hajiya Hauwa, turning to her. "What a surprise! How do you do?"

"I'm fine," said Tasidi, laughing. "We're here concerning Saudatu. We brought her *zance* chest for you to see."

"Truly? In the name of the Prophet? *Allahu Akbar*, as we hear the muezzin say! Well, I may as well get up and have a look."

Hajiya Hauwa examined the contents of the chests thoroughly, item by item, before she called Alhaji Bello to come and feast his eyes on it all.

"The women who brought the chests have said that the family is waiting to hear a response as soon as possible," said Rabi once Alhaji Bello had come in. "If their proposal is accepted, they want to make arrangements for a quick marriage. Therefore, you should tell Alhaji. I'll come back at sunset, and you can tell me what he says."

"May Allah bless the marriage," said Alhaji Bello. "God willing, I will see my brother tomorrow and call and report to you. Don't bother coming here; I will come to you myself."

"Thank you and may Allah bless you, amin."

The following morning, Alhaji Bello went to Alhaji Abdu's house and salaamed twice before leaning against the wall in the entranceway to wait for him to come out. He realized that he had not been to his brother's house for eight months, and began to wonder how this meeting would turn out. During the last meeting his brother had been abusive, derisive and contemptuous. But this time, since it was a question of marriage that brought him, he hoped the meeting would be more amicable.

Having emerged from the house, Alhaji Abdu regarded his brother with a frosty glance and a frown on his face.

Alhaji Bello ignored the unwelcoming look and bowed to greet him. "How have you spent the night, Alhaji?"

"Why are you here?" asked the other instead of returning the greeting. "I told you never to call on me again."

"Kindly allow me to tell you what brought me here. After you've heard me out, if it doesn't go down well with you, you can send me away. After all, you didn't invite me to come."

"Quickly tell me what it is all about," he said, looking at his watch. "I was on my way out."

"Rabi brought Saudatu's *zance* gifts to my house yesterday night," said Alhaji Bello with equanimity. "The girl is lucky. She's got a very wealthy man for a suitor. He wants a quick marriage, so there shouldn't be any delay. The girl has returned his love. If you approve of it, a message should be relayed to them at once."

Alhaji Bello noticed, while he was saying this, that his brother's attention seemed to be somewhere else. "Have you heard what I said?" he asked.

"What if I have? What do you want me to do about it?"

"What do you mean, Alhaji? This is your own daughter I'm talking about."

"You can all go to hell for all I care: the suitor, the girl's mother, you yourself. I have told you never to come to my house again, just as I have told her to keep her children away from me. I will have nothing to do with them. I can do without you all." After a pause, he continued. "I don't care in the slightest whether Saudatu marries or not. So long—and never salaam to me again."

He went indoors before his brother could say anything more. Alhaji Bello remained there for about ten minutes without moving. He was so upset that tears flowed from his eyes. He rubbed at them with a portion of his gown and said with a sigh, "May Allah give you the same treatment you give us."

He sat astride his motorcycle and drove away.

CHAPTER TEN

Alhaji Bello arrived at Saudatu's house at ten in the morning. He salaamed in the entranceway, where he found some young customers eating, and was given permission to go in. Inside, Rabi was serving more noisy youngsters, each of them clutching a dish they had brought along to collect the food. She called Saudatu to attend to them and spread a mat for Alhaji Bello to sit down. Saudatu briefly came and greeted him before going back to serving the customers.

Even before they exchanged greetings, Rabi suspected that all was not well; and after they had, Alhaji Bello fell silent, from which she began to guess that something awful had happened. Had Alhaji Abdu rejected the proposal? Or perhaps he had found another suitor for his daughter?

"Rabi, I've just met Alhaji Abdu..." He fell silent again, as if he didn't want to go on.

"How did it go? You look worried. If he's found another suitor for her, I don't know what I can do about it."

"He hasn't done anything like that, Rabi. He just treated me with utter contempt."

Rabi's heart began to pound, her body became slack, and she felt as if her insides had gone all topsy-turvy.

"He made me wait more than ten minutes after I arrived before he came out to see me. And then he looked at me with an expression so haughty, I can't even describe it."

"What can you do? A person's nature is like something engraved in stone."

Having told her how it had gone between him and his brother, he now tried to console her. "Don't worry about it; this marriage will come to pass. I will marry off Saudatu myself. Ask Malam Shehu to come here tonight and accompany me to deliver the news of the acceptance of the proposal. Then I'll arrange for the marriage to be solemnized."

"You know your brother. He'll be furious with you." Rabi was terribly worried.

"So what if he is? Yes, I know my brother, and he's a despicable person. Whatever the case, I am the *wali* for Saudatu's marriage now—his actions have made that very clear—and I will stand in for the role he should have filled. May Allah bless the marriage."

He got up and left.

Rabi remained motionless, fretting and biting her lips in anguish before finally spilling tears over this awful new turn of events. She prayed for retribution for the misery Alhaji Abdu had brought upon her. Then she dressed and hurriedly left the house, without even bothering to tell Saudatu where she was going. She found her brother Malam Shehu on the way back from the market with the day's provisions. Even before they greeted each other, she burst into tears.

"What's wrong?" he asked her. "What happened to you?"

"Oh, God," she wailed. "I have seen the worst of men. What is to become of me? The worst thing in life has happened to me..."

She narrated tearfully the altercation between Alhaji Abdu and Alhaji Bello on the issue of Saudatu's marriage.

"Why are you worrying so much about that?" asked Malam Shehu. "Are you mad? He divorced you already, so who cares what he says about your daughter's marriage? The most important thing is that she's found a suitor. What else is there to worry about? Brush your tears away, please!"

"How can Saudatu marry if Alhaji won't have anything to do with it? Does he mean to say she isn't his daughter? Isn't she among his heirs? Must I furnish her bridal room and buy the *gara* gift myself? Oh, I will never forgive that man. He hasn't sent us even a single naira for food since I left his house. He doesn't care in the least how we fare. Doesn't he fear Allah at all? Doesn't he think of the hereafter...?"

"If he had any fear of Allah in his heart, he surely wouldn't act the way he has been acting. Go back home; I'll see you at sunset. And don't worry. We will marry off your daughter ourselves."

Rabi returned home, where she found Kabiru. Tearfully, she told him, too, what had happened. He gave her the same advice as her brother had earlier, and then left her alone. She went on ruminating until nightfall.

The visitors from Saudatu's house arrived at Alhaji Abubakar's residence at 7:45 that evening and met him just as he was about to go out. Once they had introduced themselves, he invited them into his spacious carpeted sitting room where they were served water and soft drinks in glass tumblers. The cushioned chairs were upholstered in velvet, there was a room divider with a giant TV and VCR in it, and there were photographs covering the walls. Books, including the Holy Qur'an, filled a bookcase nearby. A pleasant perfume pervaded the whole sitting room. The callers sat in awe of the expensive furnishings as they sipped their drinks. Alhaji Abubakar left the room for a while, to give them a chance to admire the decor at their leisure.

Once he returned and they exchanged greetings, Alhaji Bello said, "We're here about the girl to whom you sent the *zance* gifts. We were told that you would prefer a quick marriage. The girl has consented, and so we have come here to inform you that your proposal to marry her has been accepted. May Allah support your efforts to lead a happy married life with her, amin."

"Amin," repeated Alhaji Abubakar, "and thank you very much. I promise to see to it that we lead a happy married life." He got up to get a piece of paper and a Biro pen, and then returned. "I have a question to ask," he said.

"Go ahead; you can ask me," said Alhaji Bello. "I am Alhaji Bello, the brother of the girl's father. This is Malam Shehu, Saudatu's maternal uncle."

"Oho, that's it then. I wanted to ask the venue where the marriage will be solemnized, as well as her father's full name."

"It will take place in my house at Soron Dinki," said Alhaji Bello. "Saudatu's father's name is Alhaji Abdu, but I am her *wali*. Is that all right with you?"

"Of course; I'm asking for the purpose of printing the invitation card, you know. Marriages should be solemnized on Sundays... Is next Sunday okay?"

Alhaji Bello turned and repeated the question to Malam Shehu.

"Next Sunday is fine," said Malam Shehu, "but there is one thing. After tying the marital knot, enough time should be allowed for the women to prepare for the wedding."

"I have no objection," said Alhaji Abubakar with a smile. "May Allah bless the marriage, amin."

"Amin," said the visitors. "We want to be on our way now."

"Thank you. Take this gift, please. You can buy some kola-nuts with it."

"Oh, no!" said Alhaji Bello. "We won't accept money! After all, we came ourselves—it's not like we're messengers to be tipped. No, it isn't done."

"Take it for the sake of Allah and His Prophet," Alhaji Abubakar begged them. "After all, you didn't ask for it; it's my own idea to give it to you. Besides, it's just *tukwici*, a token of appreciation for the good news you've brought me. I will feel slighted if you refuse to take it."

"Fine then," said Alhaji Bello. "May Allah bless you. We are very grateful for it."

Alhaji Abubakar escorted them to the place where Alhaji Bello had parked his motorcycle. As Alhaji Bello and Malam Shehu rode to Rabi's house, they didn't speak of anything else but the great respect they had been shown by the prospective son-in-law. When they got there, they related to Rabi exactly what had transpired and told her that the day had been fixed for the next week. Alhaji Bello placed before her the one hundred naira gift that Alhaji Abubakar had given them.

"I have asked him to give you some time to prepare for the wedding," said Malam Shehu.

"Fine, *yaya*," said Rabi. "Let us hope for the best. Everything depends on you."

"Rabi, don't try to take on more than you can handle. You shouldn't try to buy your daughter more than you can afford, just because she's marrying a rich man."

"He's right," said Alhaji Bello. "Don't bother yourself too much. Take that money and buy Saudatu something with it."

"Oh, no! I won't take a single kobo. It belongs to you."

"I'll take twenty naira, but that's all," said Alhaji Bello. "Think of all the expenses you have to bear."

"Me too; I'll take the same amount," said Malam Shehu. "Now we'll be on our way. You can contact us if anything comes up, so that we can pass on the news to everyone."

They left for the night, leaving Rabi with her jumble of emotions. The following morning at about ten o'clock, her sister Tasidi, who she had sent for, turned up at the house. Rabi brought her up to date on recent developments. Tasidi expressed her anger with Alhaji Abdu and her happiness with the bridegroom.

"What plans have you made for furnishing the bride's bedroom?" she asked.

"Well, it's our responsibility now, of course," said Rabi, "and things are so expensive these days! Altogether, I have seven hundred and forty naira, including my starting capital and the profits from the food selling business."

"Oh, God," said Tasidi. "That won't even buy a bed, leave alone anything else."

"Have you forgotten the money mother left us? It's still in the bank, and I've never spent even a kobo."

"Thanks be to Allah. I *had* forgotten about it. How much interest has it earned? It must be up to two thousand by now?"

"More. It's two thousand one hundred and fifty."

"No problem then. I have a lot of matching ceramic dishes, too. We can exchange those at the market to buy new sets."

"What about enamelware dishes?" Rabi asked.

"What about them? Personally, I'd rather put together something like they did for my friend Yahanasu that time."

"Oh, Tasidi. Those people are well off; we're just not in the same class. I'd prefer to go for something cheaper."

"Nowadays, nothing's cheap. Listen, you just leave everything to me."

"Oh, alright, I give up. May Allah help you succeed."

"That's what I like to hear! May He help us *all* succeed!"

The preparations continued, on both the bride's side and the groom's, up until the big day of the religious function. On Sunday the 6th of April, 1984, at 11 a.m., Alhaji Abubakar Barau and Saudatu Abdu were married. Multitudes of people turned up, and the learned mullahs proclaimed that the large crowd was a blessing. The roads around the Friday Mosque where blocked with vehicles in all four directions, and many guests had to park far off and walk to the venue. The alley leading to Alhaji Bello's house was so packed with people that giant nylon mats had to be spread by the roadside so that people could sit down before the tying of the marriage knot. Everyone prayed for Allah to bless the couple.

Three days later, a group of women delivered two more bulging boxes to the house of the bride, containing twelve cloths of atamfa, lace, and velvet, two handbags, and a *gogoro* headwrap. They met Rabi alone; Saudatu was in the inner room talking with her siblings.

"Why didn't you tell us you were coming?" Rabi asked, overwhelmed. "I'm the only one ready to receive you."

"We didn't know we would be making the visit, either," said one of the women, "otherwise we would have sent word to expect us." She added after a brief pause, "We have a message for you, which is that you shouldn't bother about furnishing the room of the bride, as Alhaji Abubakar has already made preparations for it. Also, we will come again in two days, to fix the dates for the wedding functions."

"May God see us through to that day," said Rabi. "May Allah bless us all, amin. You know, you didn't collect your *tukwici* gift when you came here last. And none of us knows where you live."

"Don't worry," said one of the women. "The gift you have given us transcends money. The fact that you are sending the girl to live with us shows you much and you trust us."

"All the same," said Rabi, "one of my boys will follow you home to see the house, so that he can show it to his elders."

Saudatu's brother Sani followed them outside, where he discovered that it was Alhaji Abubakar himself who had driven the women to the house. Alhaji Abubakar drove the women back, then retraced his route to drop the boy at home. On the way, he asked the boy, "Does your father stay with you, in the same house?"

The boy was just a boy, after all, and that was all it took: Sani revealed everything that had happened between his father and mother. Alhaji Abubakar drove slowly, so that he could hear the whole story, listening carefully to every word. When he arrived, he gave Sani a crisp new ten naira note, and asked him to call Saudatu out to meet him.

After tying the knot, a feeling of bashfulness had developed between him and her. She would smile a great deal, with her head inclined. The thought of that lovely, slightly gap-toothed smile of hers always gave him pleasant dreams at night. He recalled that on the night of the big day, he had done all the talking. She had been extremely shy and quiet throughout his visit. As for her, the soft words he had spoken that day had made her feel sure that could never live a life apart from this wonderful man. She couldn't wait to join him in his house, to serve him as a wife, to see how happy she could make him; she felt like the time left until the wedding was passing much too slowly.

Today, she came out and found him standing, the mat she had sent out for him still rolled up and leaned against the wall. When their eyes met, they smiled at one another. She knelt and greeted him.

"My bride," he said, "I don't mean to stay here. I'd like to take you on a drive into town. What do you say?"

"You give the order," she said, "and I obey. But let me go and tell them at home."

"Of course. Go ahead."

He watched her as she entered the house. *What a pleasure it will be to live with her,* he thought, *if she goes on behaving like this!* His most fervent wish was that she wouldn't ever start treating him with the sort of contempt that Hajiya Halima did. Since the day he had brought her the shopping bag of gifts to announce his impending marriage, they had not been on good terms. She had thrown the things into his sitting room and left in a huff. She had ignored him ever since, refusing to speak to him or do anything he asked her to do. Her only interaction with him was to plunk his morning tea on the table in his room. She didn't even collect money for the day's provisions from him anymore, but took it from the cook instead.

Today, before he had left the house, he had gone to Hajiya Halima's room to tell her that they had run out of detergent, but she had gone into the toilet to avoid talking to him. He was at his wits' end. It wouldn't do any good to talk to her parents. Everyone knew he had just recently split with Hajiya Amina and that a new bride was about to join him, so if he tried to lodge any complaints against Hajiya Halima now, people would say he just didn't want to live with her anymore either. He had given up on her. Anyway, whenever he visited Saudatu, she filled him with happiness. Taking her on a drive around town would go a long way to soothing his anger and letting him forget the wounded feeling his other wife had left him with.

Saudatu was delighted to be sitting there in the front seat beside him as he turned the key in the ignition. They drove away talking of romantic things while music played softly from a CD player.

Eventually, he asked her about what Sani had told him, though he did not reveal the source of his information. He told her that he had learned about her life and the problems that had cropped up between her parents. He told her that his heart went out to her mother, and that he thought the way Rabi's former husband had treated them was despicable.

Once they returned, he gave her one hundred naira and asked her to tell her mother that he would visit her the next day, and that she should arrange for someone to escort him to make social calls at the houses of Saudatu's relatives.

Then he drove back to his house; but feeling sure that if he went inside he would find some trouble there to upset him, he drove on past the gates, wandering the roads aimlessly until around midnight, when he finally returned home. The only time he felt at ease anymore was when he was with Saudatu—not even when he was away at the marketplace. That was a place for work, not for relaxation.

CHAPTER ELEVEN

"The problem with you," said Tasidi, "is that you worry too much. Let's just go!"

She and Rabi were about to go to the market and do some shopping for the bride, as the wedding was less than a week away. Rabi had withdrawn 1500 naira from the bank, even though Alhaji Bello had offered to bear the cost of the furnishings. She had bought four sets of ceramic ware—a dozen pieces each—and a set of imported enamelware dishes for serving food, as well as cutlery, tea sets and cooking pots. It was a clever dance she performed, managing to buy everything that her daughter would need while staying within her small budget—even if it wasn't all top-quality stuff.

At last the wedding began, and it went on for a whole week. It began on Sunday when Saudatu was taken to the house of a relative, where she had her hands and feet decorated with henna; on Monday, she was back at Rabi's house, and then on Tuesday, she went to Alhaji Bello's, where the bridesmaids prepared some *alibidi* snacks and served them to the groom and his friends. On Thursday, in the late afternoon, the bride was driven to the groom's house by his chauffeur, and she walked through the door holding a broom in her left hand and a kettle in the right, as per the custom. She was veiled and beautifully turned out, her limbs glowing with henna and her hair done up with pomade and tied into a bun.

Once she was in the house, Tasidi asked her to step into the bridal room right foot first, and then to sit and stretch her leg out and offer gratitude to Allah. Next her aunt asked her to unveil her face so she could see what the room looked like. She was overjoyed at the sight of the elegant and expensive furnishings, all of them in matching colours. There was a cupboard filled with ceramic vessels and a dressing mirror with bottles of make-up. Both the room and the parlour had wall-to-wall carpeting, and pictures of the bride and groom adorned all the walls. There was even an en-suite bathroom and toilet.

The realization that all these riches belonged to her came as a bit of a shock to Saudatu. Sleep is a thief, as the eloquent among the Hausa people say, yet it failed to work its magic on the bride that day. She didn't sleep a wink, but stayed up through the night chatting with two young cousins and an old aunt who had come to keep her company. In the morning, her sister Bilkisu brought porridge and bean-cakes for breakfast and tea, with bread and omelette made by the cook. At nine o'clock, the groom entered and found the bride dressing, while her aunt sat in the parlour. He stared at the bride and admired her beauty as she rubbed her body with cream, oblivious to his presence. Then, suddenly feeling that someone was watching her, she turned and was astonished to see him standing there. She blushed and tried to adjust her wrap to cover her thighs.

"You are too modest," he said. "There's no need for such shame between us, Saudatu. I just came to greet you before I go to the market."

She tilted her head forward and said, "I wish you all the best. May God prosper you."

The vision of her in her dressing room applying cream to her skin stayed on his mind for the rest of the day. What made him happiest of all was the little prayer she had said for him. Neither of his other wives had ever done that.

By late morning on Friday, the house began to fill up with women and children all in good cheer, some of them pinching their noses now and then to make joyous ululations. The relatives of the groom began cooking food in giant pots, cutting meat and cleaning rice.

But as for Hajiya Halima, ever since that Sunday, she had been so consumed with anger that she felt it would be her undoing. On this day, when women celebrants were supposed to spend the whole day with the bride, her eyes had reddened to the colour of two burning coals. However, her own relatives had warned her not to show how upset she was with her husband in public, as that might spark off gossip. So she stayed indoors throughout the day, only going out to collect her husband's dishes in his room. The expression on her face would have given her away to anyone who saw it: all the anger that was burning inside her was right there on display. She came out just long enough to ask the driver to deliver food to her husband, and then she shut herself up in her room for the night.

On Saturday, the day of the unveiling of the bride, only very close relatives turned up. The bride was bathed in the afternoon and her room was tidied up. She dressed very beautifully, and was then taken to Hajiya Halima's room so the two could be introduced, and so the new bride could be assigned to the care of the senior wife. Hajiya Halima's feelings were plain: she kept silent, frowning and glaring at the bride throughout the brief meeting. Another woman had to do the talking for her. Still another had to bring the five naira the senior wife was supposed to pay, according to custom, to get the new bride to talk. Tasidi wanted to refuse to accept the money, but the older relatives prevailed on her to prevent a quarrel.

Back in her room, the women began to counsel the bride on living in the same house with her husband, the other wife and domestic staff. They stressed that she must try her best to live amicably with her co-wife, and especially that she shouldn't allow herself to be provoked. (They had already gotten the strong impression that the senior wife would not be overfriendly.) They also advised her to abide by whatever her husband said and never to oppose him. They went home after sundown, leaving her by herself.

Having said the Magrib prayer, Saudatu heard her husband salaam and come in with Alhaji Uba, the friend of his she had met before. She modestly tilted her head down, and listened to their banter until the Isha' prayer, when they gave her the obligatory *buda-baki* shopping and went out again. She unpacked the box and found bottles of pomade, perfume, powder and soap, along with one hundred naira. She put it away. The cook came in shortly after that, and asked for dishes to serve her and her husband.

On his return, Alhaji Abubakar went straight to his room to wait for Hajiya Halima to bring his bride to him. It didn't occur to him to worry about her foul mood; he foolishly assumed that just as Hajiya Amina had brought Hajiya Halima to him on their wedding night, so Hajiya Halima would now do the same with Saudatu.

When he got tired of waiting, he went to the bride's room. He tried the handle and found the door locked.

Instead of knocking, he simply went back to his bed upstairs.

It went on like that for four days. He only met his bride in the mornings, when he left for the market. When he asked her why she kept her door locked at night, she would just keep silent. On the fifth day, before he left for the mosque at sundown, he snuck into her room and removed the keys to the door. Then, after midnight, he returned to the room.

He found her a virgin. It made him extremely happy, and she was extremely happy too.

In the morning, he sent word to her family to come and attend to her.

Rabi sent a message to Tasidi, who went to the house and cleaned her up, praising and blessing her all the while.

Alhaji Abubakar gave Saudatu's aunt Tasidi five hundred naira, and bought a new TV, VCR and refrigerator for the bride. The love between the husband and wife grew ever deeper, and so did Saudatu's peace of mind.

Thus they began to live the happy married life that everyone had prayed so hard for them to have.

But what of the father of the bride, Alhaji Abdu, and the aging prostitute he married? He didn't bother himself with any of this. Having made up his mind not to attend, he actually drove out of town on the day the marital knot was tied. His wife, Delu, was furious when she heard the news about Saudatu's marriage to a rich man; she hated to hear of any of Rabi's children coming into good fortune. It took a week before she mentioned the marriage to her husband.

"When is Saudatu's marriage?" she asked. "Or are they not talking to you about it?"

"The last I heard about it was when Alhaji Bello came to visit. It has nothing to do with me, anyway."

"It would have been better if you had handled the matter differently, Alhaji. Now I'm the one who'll be blamed for the way you acted. What do you intend to buy for the girl? You know you're supposed to buy her a bed."

"I won't be dragged into it. It's their responsibility."

"Oh Alhaji, people will hate me for this. Who's going to buy it for her if you don't?"

"I won't have anything to do with them. Not after the way they treated you."

Delu sighed, though secretly she was happy to know she still had her husband under her firm control. "Are you still standing so firm because of that minor incident? You can forgive them, as far as I am concerned."

Though happy to hear this, he said, "Let alone my previous wife and children, I would have disowned my own mother if she spoke against you. My love for you is still as fresh as always. Only God could keep you and me apart."

Of course, Delu did not think of him in quite the same way. She had the young electrician on her mind instead. They had arranged to meet that very day after her husband had left for work. But instead of leaving, Alhaji Abdu went on and on spouting meaningless talk. Finally she interrupted him, saying, "Alhaji, you'd better go to the market and earn for the day's provisions before it gets too late, don't you think?"

"All right, but by Allah I don't want to. I'd rather stay here with you! Still, I would never go against your wishes."

"Oh Alhaji, come now, you're not a child."

"I'm not being childish, I'm telling the truth. By Allah, I think I love you more than you realize."

"Well here's what you can do for me then: buy me some roast tripe on your way home. I'm craving some today."

"I'll get it for you. Roast tripe, eh? You're not pregnant, by any chance?"

"Who knows, Alhaji? After all the children you've sired already, you still want more?"

"A child of yours would be more important to me than that entire lot."

"Goodbye. I wish you all the best."

"So be it. See you later."

Had he looked carefully, he would have seen Jatau, the electrician, standing near the mosque waiting for him to leave. The youth rushed over to the house the moment Alhaji Abdu drove away. He salaamed at the doorstep. Once he came in, Delu said to him, "Why bother to salaam? You should have come straight in the moment he left."

"Oh no! It's not my own household to just barge in like that. It's better to salaam first."

"Well, you enjoy yourself better here than the head of the household does, that's for sure. I've managed to avoid his advances for four days now."

"Why not leave him if you don't love him?"

"He's just a protective shield to me, like the hedges bordering a farm. And I don't intend to leave him now, so be more careful when you come into the house. People love to poke their noses into other people's business."

As it happened, Delu's warning came too late. A roadside trader, from whom Jatau had bought cigarettes while he waited for Alhaji Abdu to leave, had been watching Jatau's comings and goings for some time. He had noticed that the electrician always seemed to visit while the head of the household was out. It had happened enough times that he had a pretty good idea what was going on between the youth and the housewife. The trader never thought of telling Alhaji Abdu about it; instead he just prayed that the man would come home early one day and find out for himself. Yet Alhaji Abdu only ever returned from work at sunset.

And so the lovers went on like this, brazenly, without the fear of Allah.

Six months after Saudatu's marriage, Alhaji Abdu was still maintaining his stand concerning Rabi and his children. He attended to his own concerns, and they attended to theirs. Meanwhile, his business continued to prosper. The stall in Sabon Gari Market was always full of goods, and he had large numbers of customers every day. Like most of his fellow businessmen, he kept his money locked in a drawer at his stall, rather than trust it to the bank.

CHAPTER TWELVE

Life soon changed a great deal at the house of Alhaji Abubakar, because truth and lies cannot go on existing side by side for long.

Within two weeks of her arrival, Saudatu began to have altercations with Hajiya Halima. The latter had been spoiling for a fight, but the former tried her best to ignore it. The next time it was the new bride's turn to cook, Hajiya Halima refused to hand over the responsibility to her and cooked for two days longer than she should have. Only after that did she let Saudatu take over.

Alhaji Abubakar called the two wives together to give them a talk on looking after the house. The senior wife showed up only reluctantly, and barely paid attention to what he was saying. He was used to her attitude and didn't make an issue of it right then. Afterwards, though, he called her for a talk in private.

"Hajiya Halima, I will not have you go on behaving the way you did when Hajiya Amina was still around. I will hold you responsible for whatever happens. That girl is a newcomer; she doesn't know what goes on in this house. If you maintain your dignity, she will never hold me in contempt. But if you don't, I will never have any peace of mind. For the sake of God and his Prophet, let's try to live together in peace."

She said, "Oh, Alhaji, why hold me responsible? I don't have anything to do with your new bride. We're both married to you, but that's as far as it goes. You should be telling this to her, not me."

"You don't understand. If you treat me with contempt in front of her, she'll learn to treat me that way too."

"I don't treat you with contempt. And how she relates to you is her own business."

"So it only concerns me and her, and you have nothing to do with it? And you'll go on refusing to do anything I ask you to do? Fine, I don't care. Do whatever you like. But by Allah, if you cause her any harm, I'll divorce you. I approached you to talk to you in peace, but you've spurned me. Since you have no manners, you can go."

"So you only called me here to disrespect me," she said, bursting into tears. "What have I done to you? Go ahead, divorce me; you don't have to wait for me to do anything to her. You can give me the divorce paper now. I guess you married her so you could get rid of me. Fine, thank you very much. I'll be waiting for the paper."

She stormed out and went downstairs. From then on, she stopped talking to anyone in the house—though she went on serving him his tea every morning. She kept to her room and the bride kept to hers. The two of them did not speak at all. When Saudatu asked her husband why her co-wife wouldn't return her greetings, he just asked her to ignore it.

One day when it was Saudatu's turn to oversee the cooking, she was in the kitchen helping the cook when Hajiya Halima came in to boil some water for her flask. The water boiled, and as Hajiya Halima was pouring it, Saudatu, who had just peeled some yams and was carrying them in a dish to the sink to wash them, slipped on a peel that had fallen on the floor. The heavy dish of yams flew from her grasp and hit Hajiya Halima's arm. The pot of hot water she was holding crashed to the ground, spilling all the water in it. Her flask fell to the floor as well and broke. The cook stood there, watching everything.

"Sorry," said Saudatu, getting up quickly. "I slipped on a yam peel. I hope you weren't hurt?"

As soon as Hajiya Halima got to her feet, she gave Saudatu a violent slap. Saudatu held her cheek in shock and kept mum as the senior wife began to scream at her.

"Bitch! Try to burn me, will you? You stupid villager, rushing around like an idiot because you're so excited to have some food!"

Saudatu wasn't sure whether she should wrestle Hajiya Halima and throw her to the ground; slap her back, to show her she was no coward; or just turn around and march home to her family. Before she could make up her mind and act, she watched her adversary walk away, leaving the broken pieces of the flask and the upturned pot lying there on the ground.

"Please don't get upset," said the cook. "Hajiya is rash and troublesome; she used to always fight with the other wife who left the house, too. Don't let her..."

Before he could finish, Saudatu ran out of the kitchen crying tears of anger and rage. She didn't know what she had done to deserve the slap. She wished she had taken the chance to slap her back. She was still crying when she heard her husband return and go straight to his room.

The cook, once he was finished with the meal, knocked on her door to collect the serving dishes for her husband. She ignored him and he went back to the kitchen. Some moments later, he returned, salaamed outside the door, and asked for the dishes again, only to be told that she didn't have any.

Then her husband called her over the intercom. Instead of answering the summons she ignored him, too, and went on crying. He came down, wondering what was wrong, as she had never failed to answer him before. He had rung the bell three times. The cook told him that he hadn't been able to get the dishes from the new bride, either. Alhaji Abubakar went in and found Saudatu lying in bed, sobbing. Instantly outraged at whoever had provoked her to tears, he lifted her up, only to see that her eyes were red and puffy. He sat on the bed, his body shivering with worry.

"What happened, Saudatu? Why are you crying?"

She refused to answer him at first. After he rested her head on his lap, she spoke. "I won't stay in this house any longer," she said, crying. "Take me back to my family." She got up to go to her wardrobe.

"Sit down," he said, drawing her back to the bed. "Tell me what happened. Who made you so upset? Or are you not well?"

She narrated what had happened between her and Hajiya Halima, and told him that if he didn't believe her, he could go ask the cook.

The head of the household went to the kitchen in a huff and heard the cook's version, which was enough of a confirmation. Then he went on to Hajiya Halima's room.

"Halima, what made you slap Saudatu?"

"She spilled some yams on me."

"What do you think she is, your slave? It was an accident. She slipped."

"She did it on purpose. She even broke my flask. I'm not her slave, either."

"It wasn't on purpose. The cook said you slapped her even after she apologized to you. Why did you do it?"

"I'm of no value to you. I guess now that you've married the daughter of someone big and important, I don't matter to you anymore," Hajiya Halima said sarcastically.

"You have no manners. You slapped her for no good reason, and still you have the temerity to talk like this. What do you mean by it?"

"I mean you can go ahead and hit me on her behalf, since *she's* somebody's daughter, and *I'm* just the child of a donkey. You always side with..."

He slapped her violently before she finished saying what she wanted to say. The force of the blow threw her to the ground. Then he kicked her, hard enough that she rolled on the floor. Yet she didn't spill a single teardrop; she only shook all over. He pulled her up and into the family compound and then pushed her towards her room.

"That was for what you did to her," he said. "What are you going to do about it, you worthless, frivolous woman? I said what are you going to do about it? Pack your things and leave my house. I won't tolerate your rudeness anymore. Leave the keys to your room before you go and don't let me see you in this house tomorrow morning. Otherwise I'll throw your belongings into the street."

He stormed out of the house feeling furious, and drove aimlessly around for a while before parking at a food stall. He ordered five bottles of soft drink and sat in his car sipping them until 10:30 p.m. He got back home at 10:45 p.m. and ordered his guards to lock up. He found Saudatu in her room watching TV with Shamsuddeen, the young son of the wife who'd just been sent away, strapped to her back. His heart went out to her, seeing her like this: she was carrying on her back the child of the woman who had abused her. He touched her to get her attention. "Did you tie him on your back because he refused to go to sleep?"

"He wouldn't stop crying after she left. I picked him up because she had locked his *kamu* in her room, and he was hungry for it."

"Where did she leave him? Did she bring him to you?"

Recalling what had happened between her and the child's mother after her husband had left the house, she nodded and kept quiet. She knew it would only make him angrier to hear how Hajiya Halima had thrown her child at Saudatu, telling her to hand Shamsuddeen over to his "lunatic of a grandmother."

"Tell that man I've gone for good," she had said. "He can try and prevent me from marrying again if he dares. As for you—you're the child of a mother who's a pauper and a father who divorced her to marry a whore. Why don't you ask your mother to come marry Alhaji as well, and come and stay with you both. As for that child, you can cook him and eat him for all I care."

Saudatu didn't know what Hajiya Halima had meant by calling her husband's mother a lunatic. In any case, she couldn't bring herself to relay the message. She just said that the child had gone to Hajiya Halima's room crying, and the guards had told Saudatu that the child's mother had left in a taxi. Her husband guessed that she was hiding something, for he knew there was no way Hajiya Halima would have left so quietly. But after several failed attempts to make Saudatu tell him what really happened, he gave up.

He got the key and went into Hajiya Halima's room, where he collected the child's clothes, tins of food, and feeding bottles, and handed them over to Saudatu, who suddenly found herself in the role of a nursing mother. Shamsuddeen spent a full month with her before his grandparents persuaded Alhaji Abubakar to let Hajiya Halima back into his house.

When she did, she continued to behave as badly as before—in fact even worse. The moment she came back she unceremoniously snatched the baby from Saudatu without even a word of thanks. Later, when Alhaji Abubakar came in to share some biscuits he'd bought and asked Saudatu where the boy was, she told him that the baby's mother had taken him back. She bowed her head as she said it, averting her eyes, and he could see that his young wife was trying to hide tears. Deciding he didn't need to discuss it with Hajiya Halima first, he told Saudatu, "It looks like you've gotten used to spending the night with the baby. Should I bring him back to you?"

"No, let her keep him," she said. "She mocked me—she told me I should bear a child of my own."

"Is that what she said? Well. If it would make you happy to have a child for company, we can adopt a girl to come stay with you. Would you like that? Or perhaps one of your cousins would send one of their children to come live with you?"

"None of them will agree to it."

"I can bring Ummi to you, my four-year-old daughter. Would you like to have her?"

"Of course I would, but surely her mother wouldn't agree?"

"She's the daughter of my first wife, who bore me three children. Ummi is the first, then Baba. Both of them stay with my mother. The youngest, Jamila, is still with her mother, since she is nursing, but I will take her back once she is weaned."

Once he had explained all this, and Saudatu had agreed to the arrangement, Alhaji Abubakar immediately left for his parents' house. But there he came face to face with another unhappy incident: Hajiya Fatima had suffered a relapse and become hysterical again.

Four local mullahs were busy praying for her as she lay in bed talking in feverish delirium. His father sat nearby, looking glum. Alhaji Abubakar rushed over to his mother and asked her what was wrong, but she just continued muttering, seemingly oblivious to his presence. His father explained that it had begun after the Magrib prayer. Alhaji Abubakar stayed with them till midnight, despite his father's insistence that he go home. He forgot all about taking Ummi back with him. The sick woman finally fell asleep at a quarter to one, and her son left for home.

He went up to his room and got into bed, but found it impossible to get to sleep. At 5:30 in the morning, he went back to his parents' house, where he found his mother still asleep. He hung around until she woke up. When she did, she seemed to have no recollection of having talked nonsense all through the previous night.

"What's wrong?" she asked her son. "What brings you here so early in the morning?"

"How did you sleep last night?" Alhaji Abubakar greeted her. Her husband came in before she could respond.

"How do you feel?" he asked her on seeing her sitting down. "Have you said your prayers? Don't you think you should?"

"What happened, Alhaji? I woke up and saw my boy sitting here with me." She inclined her head and asked, "Did I have another attack of my mental illness?"

"Just go and pray," said Alhaji Barau. "No need for empty talk."

Hajiya Fatima went and prayed, and received the greetings of friends and visitors. Then she was left alone with her husband and son. "Go on to the market, now," she said to her son. "I feel much better now, thank God."

It was then that Alhaji Barau explained to his son for the first time the story of how she had been stricken ill. The memories made him shed tears.

Then Alhaji Abubakar's mother asked him whether Hajiya Halima had returned to his house. Anger welled up inside him at the sound of her name; he took a few moments to let it subside, and then narrated what had transpired between him and his second wife.

"I wanted to hand Ummi over to my new bride, but I changed my mind because of your illness," he finished.

"Wouldn't it be asking too much of her? Saudatu is hardly more than a girl herself."

"Don't forget, mother, that she looked after Shamsuddeen for a month before his mother took him away. By Allah, I have no doubt that she can be responsible for the girl."

"No, I don't agree. Didn't you say you wanted to enrol Ummi in a school? You had better let her remain here with us."

"I have already promised Saudatu," said her son. "But I'll ask her to be patient."

"You had better let him take her away," said Alhaji Barau, who had been pulling his prayer beads. "He has said that they can look after her. The owner of a room knows best where it leaks."

"If she stays with us," said her son, "I don't have to come here every day to take her to school."

His mother said, "I was worried about handing Ummi over to your new wife, but since you seem set on it, I won't forbid it. I suppose you're trying to appease her."

"It isn't that; it's just that I know she's a serious-minded, capable woman. You should have seen the way she took care of Shamsuddeen."

"You can take her with you." Turning to the girl, she said, "So Ummi, it looks like you'll spend tonight at your father's house! Let me pack your things."

The girl, who had just woken up, looked around her, while her grandfather continued pulling his beads. Hajiya Fatima made as if to get up, but Alhaji Abubakar asked her not to bother, as he could come back in the afternoon to pick up the girl.

When he did, he brought his new bride with him, and his mother said to Saudatu, "Saude, can you look after the girl for him? You know how children are; you have to be patient with them. We are entrusting her to you in the name of Allah and His Prophet, so take care."

"I will, Baba; I know that I can and will look after her in trust."

Hajiya Fatima's husband noticed the look of delight on his wife's face at being called 'Baba', the term for a respected parent. Before Saudatu, none of the old woman's son's wives had called her that; they had all called her Hajiya. It did a lot to endear the girl to her.

CHAPTER THIRTEEN

Near the end of 1984, the people of Kano witnessed a catastrophe that plunged them into despair. Thousands watched as their worldly riches disappeared into thin air. Many were plunged into poverty and ruin. For those who lacked faith, it seemed like the end of life itself. It was the biggest disaster in Kano since the insurrection of 1980, when the extremist Maitatsine attempted to take over the whole state, and so many Muslims lost their lives. Yet as Allah promised his Prophet Mohammed (P.B.U.H.), until the Day of Judgment, if even ten people were to survive and turn to Him for deliverance, the world would not end... It is true that in the times of Jahiliyya, the days of ignorance before the revelation of the Holy Qur'an, some people perished because of their misdeeds, as in the stories of the Prophets Nuh and Lut. But that was before Allah's promise.

What happened was this: An accidental fire burned down the Sabon Gari Market in Kano, the largest in the state.

The traders and stall-owners had never seen anything like it before. Some of them rushed into the conflagration in an effort to save their goods, but were either knocked out from smoke inhalation or perished in the inferno.

Many others had to be held back to prevent them from jumping in. The air was filled with their deafening cries, wails and prayers. A lucky few were able to snatch some of their goods from the flames, but many others lost everything. Not only the doors and window-frames but the walls themselves were burnt to ashes. It took a long time and a great number of firefighters before the blaze was extinguished.

Just as Allah may come to the aid of those who suffer afflictions, just as He gives riches and grants forgiveness, He can also take away. Alhaji Abdu happened to be among those who lost their stalls. He lost everything to the flames. The fire started either late that night or just at dawn: God alone knows the truth. It was first noticed by people who lived nearby when they woke up. Some traders only came to know about it when they arrived for work in the morning.

Alhaji Abdu left his house that day at ten o'clock. He saw people running in the direction of the market, but didn't bother to ask why. When he reached Plaza Cinema he noticed the acrid smell of smoke and saw the cloud billowing into the sky. He drove on until he got to the 'Yankura Roundabout, where he heard people shouting. The road ahead was filled with a crowd whose loud wails were drowned out by the roar of the flames. He tried to drive up close to his stall and park his car outside the Bata showroom like he usually did, but he wasn't allowed beyond the filling station near Kroda Hospital; the police had stopped onward traffic. He got out of his car and joined the crowd, some of whom were standing and watching, while others rushed back and forth carrying merchandise in their hands or on their heads. As he tried to shove his way through the throng, he caught sight of someone who had a stall close to his own, and grabbed hold of him. He asked him about the condition of his stall.

"Alhaji Abdu," said the man, "try to keep calm. All the stalls around your station have been reduced to ashes. No one can even..."

Alhaji Abdu sprinted towards the market without waiting to hear the rest, praying as he ran along. He kept bumping into people but didn't bother to look back. All he could think of was trying to salvage as much of his merchandise as he could, as he saw the other people around him doing. Yet there was no way he could reach his stall without perishing in the blazing fire. When he finally caught sight of the ruins of the stalls close to his, he lost consciousness and slumped to the ground. He was pulled aside, and it wasn't until half an hour later, when someone brought him to by splashing water on him, that he found he'd been left in front of a shop. He began crying and wailing uncontrollably, heedless of the attempts of the people around him to calm him down. He went on like that until sundown.

Yet more was still to come.

In his haste to reach his stall, he had forgotten to lock his car, thereby virtually handing it over as a gift for car thieves. When he finally went back and discovered that it was gone, he was so distressed that he passed out for a second time. He came to with the realization that packed in the trunk of the car was a full load of his and Delu's laundry. Other than two sets at home and the clothes he was wearing, he had lost everything. He had no car; no stall; no merchandise; no money. He gave a long groan, and lost consciousness for the third time. He was roused with water once more.

Just then Alhaji Bello happened by with a group of people who were helping him carry his goods to safety. Other than about two hundred naira worth of merchandise which had been singed, he hadn't lost anything. The small stall filled with goods that he owned jointly with his business partners had somehow survived the fire. He saw the condition that Alhaji Abdu was in, but walked on ahead, ignoring him. His friends protested, though; unaware of what had happened between the two of them, they persuaded him that he couldn't abandon his own brother. As the eloquent among the Hausa people say, a relative always stays close to you, no matter how far he falls.

Alhaji Bello hailed a taxi and took his brother to the hospital, asking a friend to stay and guard his goods. The taxi cut through the onlookers and sped to Murtala Hospital where a doctor admitted Alhaji Abdu. Alhaji Bello went and bought some pills for him. The patient was given a few injections, but he couldn't swallow the pills, which had to be crumbled and mixed with liquid before they could be fed to him. Alhaji Abdu soon fell asleep, after which his brother and his friends went to his house to relay the news of the incident.

They had to salaam twice before Delu came out, and when she did she wasn't even wearing a headscarf. After exchanging greetings, Alhaji Bello told her about the fire and her husband being in the hospital, but not about the loss of the stall and the car. They left her clapping her hands in shock.

Delu dressed quickly and set off for the hospital, accidentally leaving Ladidi, who was having a bath, locked inside the house. She located her husband's bed and stayed there watching him for three hours until after the Asr prayer, when she suddenly remembered the girl she had left at home. She rushed back in a hurry, picked up Ladidi, and returned to the room. She spent the night in the hospital after sending the girl to Alhaji Bello's house.

Alhaji Abdu didn't seem to recognize anybody until mid-way through the following day. Delu had just left, saying she wanted to go home and make food for them.

Shortly afterwards he began to weep, recalling the loss he had suffered in the fire, and loudly wishing that he was dead. When Delu came back, she had to force the food into him. He ended up eating only a tiny bit of the gruel she had brought along. Then she asked him what had happened, and he burst into tears.

"Delu... Delu, I have lost my stall in the fire, I have lost all my merchandise... I've lost about sixty thousand naira, and my car was stolen, too. Oh Delu..."

"The stall was burned down, Alhaji?" Delu shouted. "The car was stolen? Oh, *inna lillahi wa inna ilaihi raji'una*... from Allah we came and to Him we shall return! What terrible news! Is it really true? The stall was burned down?"

Her husband simply lay in bed and wept. Delu had nothing else to say, so she kept quiet. She kept just looking up at him, and then looking down again. Finally she sighed and asked, "So you don't have a stall, and you don't have a car. Then what do we do?"

"What can I do, Delu?" asked her husband. "All my money is gone."

"Is that so?" she asked, looking at him appraisingly.

"It's true, Delu. At least if I had some money left, I could set up a table and get back into business as a small-time trader."

"A small-time trader!? Alhaji! So we're that destitute now, are we? What a tragedy this is for us!"

"I still have the house and my fridge and TV, but I only have three sets of clothes left—the rest were in the trunk of the car." He sighed and continued, "By Allah, I think I'm ruined, Delu. Oh God, what will I do?"

"Yes, you're ruined, all right. And what about me? My clothes were lost too, along with yours."

He looked at her in astonishment. "So you think you've suffered as great a loss as I have, do you?"

"Of course I have! Those atamfas were expensive. How will I ever replace them?"

"Your *atamfas*?" he shouted. "Do you have even the slightest idea of what I lost today? Your lousy atamfas were hardly worth five hundred naira!"

"Don't shout at me. I wouldn't have given you the laundry if I'd known how it would turn out. I'm not the culprit here."

"Is it really only your clothes you're worried about? You're not bothered in the least about what happened to me, about the condition I'm in? After everything I've done for you, all you have to say is 'I'm not the culprit'? Oh Delu, how can you be so selfish?"

"Good night," she said. "I'll be on my way. I leave you to rant to yourself."

She went away quickly, in a pique. The other patients, who had witnessed everything, now watched as Alhaji Abdu shed tears like a child. Delu never bothered to call at the hospital again. She sent Ladidi to take him food instead.

Four days later Alhaji Abdu was discharged. He walked all the way home, buffeted by strong gusts of wind. When he reached his neighbourhood, several of his neighbours saw him and came to meet him. He seemed changed; he had gone thin around the neck, like a pauper. They walked to his house with him, sharing their sympathies.

But his troubles weren't over. There was still more in store for him at home.

He went straight to Delu's room without a salaam or even clearing his throat. He found her door closed, and at first he thought she wasn't in, but then he noticed that the door was unlocked. He had just started to push it open when he heard her voice, telling someone to get dressed quickly and leave in case her husband came back home.

He listened for just a moment longer to make absolutely sure that someone really was there with her. Then he drew back silently, and called some of the neighbours from outside. He explained his suspicions to them, and four of them went into the house together. One of them picked up a pestle on the way in, and another grabbed a piece of firewood. The head of the household led them to Delu's room and knocked on the door.

"Who's there?" Delu asked.

He didn't answer her at first, just knocked again. Finally he said, "It's me, Alhaji. Open the door."

She uttered a startled oath that all the men heard, but still she failed to come out. Then they began to bang on the door until it broke open. Two men burst in, came out holding a flustered-looking Jatau, and then fell on him with the pestle and firewood. His shouts of terror attracted more people to the house, which was lucky for him—the ordeal might well have proved fatal otherwise. One of the newcomers intervened to save him, but not before Jatau took a blow from the stick of firewood to his right eye. He had come into the house walking on two feet, but had to be dragged out like the carcass of a dog. He was thrown into the roadside to be cursed by passersby. By the Zuhr noontime prayer, news of the incident had travelled all around the neighbourhood and beyond. Jatau slunk away home, with children following behind him, pelting him with stones.

Delu remained closeted and crying in her room. Her husband stayed on her doorstep neither lambasting her nor beating her. "So you were carrying on behind my back this whole time, Delu? Have I ever failed to give you anything you asked of me? You took me for all the money you could get. Even the bed you sleep on in this house, I bought for you. You don't eat corn or millet, but rice, yams and spaghetti. I divorced my wife and left her nine children because of you. Now look at what I've lost in a single day. All of a sudden, I've become a pauper. And you wouldn't even bring me food in the hospital! Come out of there now, and leave my house. I won't raise a finger against you; I will leave it to Allah to judge between us. But I will hold this betrayal against you forever. Send someone to collect your belongings."

Within three months, he had forgotten all about her.

CHAPTER FOURTEEN

Rabi heard about the fire the day it happened. Her children rushed in and told her that Sabon Gari Market had gone up in flames.

"May Allah lessen the damage," was all she said. In the afternoon, a creditor of hers, Alhaji Ado, turned up and offered condolences to her. Unable to make sense of this, she asked him, "What are you consoling me for? What happened?"

"Don't tell me you don't know what has happened!" said Alhaji Ado. "Don't you know that Alhaji Abdu's stall has been reduced to ashes in the fire at Sabon Gari Market?"

It took a moment for the news to sink in, and then Rabi jumped suddenly to her feet and began dancing, cheering, and shouting for joy. She stomped her foot on the ground before resuming her seat. "Allahu Akbar! You don't know how I prayed—"

"Hear me out before you say too much," said Alhaji Ado. "While he was at the fire, his car was stolen. To tell a long story short, he's left with nothing: no shop and no car. Right now he's in a hospital bed. He hardly even knows where he is."

"Oh, God is great," said Rabi. "Thanks be to Allah! O God, today I can die happy! You have interceded on my behalf. I was abandoned and forgotten, but now I no longer hold anything against anybody!"

"Right... so perhaps it's a good time to settle your quarrel, then. You can buy some fruits or something and visit him at the hospital."

"You must be joking! Am I the one that put him there? It is Allah's will. Since Alhaji never appreciated His blessings before, he should thank Him now for what He has inflicted on him."

Rabi spent the day in an exceptionally good mood, happily offering thanks to Allah for having finally taught Alhaji Abdu a lesson. Even before he lost his riches, that money hadn't done anything to improve the lot of her and her children. So as far as she was concerned, this was divine retribution, made plain for all the world to see. She made sure that all her children—except for Saudatu—heard about the incident, but was careful not to let them see how happy it had made her.

She visited Saudatu the next day and found her lying sick in bed, as she was in the early stages of pregnancy. She had now been married for about seven months, during which time there hadn't been a single misunderstanding her and her husband. Alhaji Abubakar, whenever he met Rabi or Tasidi, would thank them profusely.

During one of Rabi's visits to his house, Hajiya Halima overheard him say to her, "Baba, I have never married a woman as sensible as Saudatu. I've never had to tell her anything more than once in the whole time she's been here."

Hajiya Halima had puffed up so full of anger that she felt as if she would burst. Her husband didn't appreciate anything she did for him! So she had failed to measure up to Saudatu, had she?

On her husband's return from the market that day, she had followed him to his room and given him an earful about the comment she had overheard. As soon as she had finished her rant and gone back downstairs, Alhaji Abubakar had picked up a paper and a Biro pen and written her a triple divorce letter. He'd gone down and asked her to hand over Shamsuddeen and all his clothes, and then given her the piece of paper. He had taken the boy and entrusted him to Saudatu. She had started to protest, but he asked her not to interfere with his decision.

Three months later he had found a young Yoruba nanny for Shamsuddeen, and also took his youngest daughter back from Hajiya Amina and brought her home. Ummi began going to a nursery school at Tarauni, and the youngest two stayed with Saudatu. Over the next three months, he didn't hear a single complaint from the children about Saudatu, who was warm and nurturing with them, treating them with fairness and honesty. Then Saudatu became pregnant herself, and he engaged another woman to help her with the household chores.

When Rabi came that day, she told her daughter about the fire.

"I am very happy to hear that," said Saudatu. "I won't go visit him."

"You foolish girl," her mother said, trying her best to sound disapproving. "One shouldn't be thankful to hear of a tragedy. He is your father, after all!"

"Oh Baba, but think of what he did to you! He doesn't deserve sympathy for what's befallen him."

"You shouldn't bother about what he did to me. He didn't do it to you. I don't want you to feel any animosity towards him."

"I am sorry, Baba. But he's been so horrible—he didn't even furnish my room for my wedding."

"Shh, better not to let people hear about it and mock you for it. No one will know he didn't if you don't tell them. Anyway, he's your father, and you can't deny that. He didn't always act so badly. You had better stop talking like that, do you hear me?"

"I won't mention anything to Alhaji, Baba."

"Don't; it isn't necessary. I should be on my way. See you later."

"Baba, take this meat for my sisters. It was bought yesterday."

"I'd rather not be seen taking something away from this house. Why not give it to the children instead?"

"Don't worry, we have a lot of it. This is my share. The children's share is in that *fanteka* dish."

Rabi packed the meat in a carry bag and took leave of Saudatu. She set off for the house of her brother, Malam Shehu, who had just returned home with the day's provisions when she got there. She related the incident of the fire to him and, because men and women think differently, he sympathized with her former husband. Seeing the depth of her brother's feelings, she went on to say, "Don't bother to go and commiserate with him; we shouldn't care what happens to him. He brought it all upon himself."

"Be reasonable, Rabi. Even if you didn't have any children by him, you shouldn't say such a thing. He is a Muslim to whom something tragic has happened, and we should have sympathy for him."

"Has he ever shown any sympathy for his children? Not one bit! That's why we're not bothered about what happens to him."

"You should consider the future, too, not only the present. Let the past be in the past."

Rabi left, went home, and shared the meat among all the children, keeping some aside for Kabiru and Ibrahim.

The next day, she called at Tasidi's house in Karkasara.

"Glad tidings," she joked to Tasidi, "but I will only tell you my news if you give me something juicy in return."

"What important news is that?" asked Tasidi, joining in the joke. "Saudatu has a while to go before she delivers her baby, so that can't be it. But I can tell from the look on your face it must be good. I'll give you two naira to tell me the news."

"Only two naira? You badly undervalue my story! By Allah, what I've got to tell you is worth at least ten."

"You wouldn't smile like that unless it was something that really must be heard. Fine, I'll give you five naira for it."

Rabi narrated everything that had happened, and it made Tasidi cheer and laugh so loud that her husband came out to see what was going on. When she told him, he began to talk about divine retribution, adding that Allah would be beneficent and merciful to those who seek His forgiveness.

Three days later, Rabi heard about what Delu had done to Alhaji Abdu, and felt so happy she could have poured water on the ground and lapped it up. She was thankful to Allah for cutting Alhaji Abdu down to size. His disrespect had scarred her; now he had acquired some scars of his own.

And yet, three months later, she began to feel pity. She felt especially sorry for him when she heard that he had been reduced to begging for his food. She became very concerned about his plight, and mentioned it on one of her visits to Saudatu's house. Rabi had to plead with her before she agreed to send her father some money to help him out. Saudatu promised to collect some money from her husband and send it to Rabi, who would then send it to Alhaji Abdu.

"Please Alhaji, I want some money," Saudatu asked her husband when he came in later in the day.

"You want to buy something with it?" he asked.

Saudatu realized that it would do no good to hide the truth anymore, so she told him everything. He was angry at being kept in the dark for so long. She explained that because her father had divorced her mother, she hadn't thought it was necessary to tell him.

"But he is still your father! That was very foolish of you. You should have informed me about it long before."

In the morning, he packed three sets of clothes and took them together with two hundred naira to Rabi's house, so that one of her boys could escort him to Alhaji Abdu's house. Sani took him there. They found Alhaji Abdu sitting on a mat in his entranceway and exchanged greetings with him.

"I'm sorry, but who are you?" asked Alhaji Abdu. "This boy looks like one of my children, but I don't recognize you."

"I am Alhaji Abubakar, Saudatu's husband." He noticed a slight change in the man before him. "She sent me here to bring you two hundred naira. As for my part, I'd like to present these clothes to you, as a gift." He pushed the package and the money over to him.

Alhaji Abdu looked his son-in-law over, noticing the quality of his clothing. "Did she ask you to bring these...?" Tears began to flow; he put up his hand to rub them away.

"Don't cry," said Alhaji Abubakar. "It's not something to cry about. It was only last night that I heard about what happened to you. Otherwise I would have done something about it before."

"I don't hold it against her or her mother for not telling you. If one could exchange one's father for another, by Allah, they'd have every right to trade me in."

He wept like a young boy for some time. Finally he fell silent.

"Be patient," said Alhaji Abubakar, overcome with emotion. "Allah remains in full control. It isn't something to shed tears about. I will see what I can do."

He left in a hurry, without saying goodbye.

Four weeks later, Alhaji Abdu was still in a severe depression, doing nothing but thinking things over and over. Every day he felt the urge to visit his brother, Alhaji Bello, but couldn't quite get himself out of the house. Finally he went there one day at sunset and found him at home. He salaamed, and sat down when he heard someone return his salaam. He recalled the fight they had had on the day he divorced Rabi, and the harsh words they had exchanged.

Alhaji Bello came out, and when he saw that it was his brother he went back for a mat. He spread it on the ground for him, thinking as he did so that he probably wouldn't have received the same treatment if he had called at Alhaji Abdu's house.

"I am here," said Alhaji Abdu, "to beg you, in the name of Allah and His Prophet, to forget everything that happened between us. I beseech you, in the name of Allah, to forgive me for everything I said to you. You know well that there is no one closer to me than you. Forgive me. For the sake of brotherhood."

"All right," said Alhaji Bello half-heartedly. "May Allah forgive us all."

His brother observed his reluctance, and he understood the reason for it, too. He waited, but when his brother didn't say anything else, he went on. "I also beg you, for the sake of Allah, to go to my former wife and apologize to her and her people on my behalf, and plead with her to come back to my house. I don't know what else I can do."

Alhaji Bello still didn't commit himself by saying anything.

"Everything in this world happens as it is fated," Alhaji Abdu continued. "There is nothing a man can do if Allah strikes him with an affliction. But whatever happens, family is still family."

Alhaji Bello give his brother a hard look. "So it seems you've finally realized that I am your brother. I thought you had decided I was a nobody. Do you think I'm some kind of fool to go and fetch your wife back for you? Have you forgotten what you told me at your house when I went to try to reconcile you with her? No, I will have nothing to do with it. You can go try and bring her back yourself. I'm not your errand boy." He got up and said, "I know you don't have anything left to live on. The only reason you want her back is so you can have someone to depend on. Go ahead then, try and get her. I'll see you later."

He went inside, leaving his visitor sitting there on the mat. Alhaji Abdu got up, sent the mat in, and left.

Three days later, on a Friday, Alhaji Abdu mustered the courage to go to Rabi's place in Rimin Kira.

Rabi had just finished saying her prayers. She hadn't yet rubbed the dust off her forehead when Sani rushed in, saying, "Baba, by Allah, our father has come! He says he wants to speak to you."

She put on her veil and found him squatting humbly in the entranceway. He exchanged greetings with her and asked after all his children. Rabi said, "Kabiru is attending the university; Ibrahim will join him this year; Saudatu is married; Bilkisu is at home for the school holidays; the other four children are going to primary school; and the youngest one still stays with me at home."

After a short silence, Alhaji Abdu began speaking in a respectful tone. "One needs patience in this world, Rabi," he started.

"Now look," Rabi interrupted him. "Don't ever come to my house again. If you do, I'll report you to the police. I will no longer have anything to do with you. Let each of us go our own way."

"Wait, Rabi. Listen…"

She went back inside abruptly and left him squatting there holding his chin in his hand. He got up, but couldn't decide whether he should stay or go; he was still hoping that she might come out again. Finally, he gave up and left. Before he had made his way out of the alley, he bumped into Kabiru, who was coming back from college. The boy, who had not seen his father for about eight months, was astonished to meet him. The last time he had seen him was when he drove past as the boy was buying some detergent to do his own washing. Kabiru was struck, now, by his father's emaciated look, but he passed him wordlessly and made to continue on his way.

Alhaji Abdu called out to the boy. "Kabiru, where are you coming from?"

He looked as glad to see his son as if the boy had been lost and he had just found him.

"From the university," said Kabiru.

He turned to go, but his father stopped him. He told him of the tragedy that had befallen him, and the way Rabi had reacted to his efforts to make peace with her.

"Please," he said, "go and beg her to be understanding and come back to me. Not just for my sake, but for your own."

Kabiru smiled and said, "If it's for our sake, Baba, there's no need for her to go back to you. We've all gotten on fine without you. I still remember trying to stop you from beating her. I still remember how you threw us out—all of us, including her. Well, Allah still loves us, even if you don't."

"Is that what you will say, too, Kabiru? Oh, what do you want me to do? Can't you let bygones be bygones? It's as though everyone I approach just treats me like a homeless madman!"

Kabiru didn't bother to keep listening. He left him standing there, talking to no one in particular. Finally Alhaji Abdu got tired of talking and fell silent. He remained standing there, thinking, until suddenly he swooned and fell into the gutter. He suffered cuts on his lips, face and ears; his face was soon covered with blood. He tried desperately to stand up but couldn't. Children gathered around and jeered at him, thinking he was a drug addict.

A little later, Sani came out to run an errand and saw the condition his father was in. He rushed back home and called Kabiru, and two boys went out to the alley together. After trying to revive their father and getting no response, Kabiru sent Sani to get a taxi. He removed the fallen man's clothes and handed them to Rabi, who burst into tears. She wanted to follow them, but Kabiru asked her to stay at home. They left for the hospital while Rabi went back indoors carrying the soiled clothes.

CHAPTER FIFTEEN

Saudatu was in Alhaji Abubakar's sitting room when she heard Bilkisu come in. When she looked up at her, she saw that she was crying. Saudatu was suddenly struck with the fear that Rabi was dead. It took her a supreme effort to ask, "What's wrong, Bilki? What happened? Has Baba fallen ill?"

Her husband had just come out of the toilet when he heard her ask the question.

"No," said Bilkisu, "she sent me to tell you that our father isn't well. He's been taken to hospital."

"What's wrong with him?" Alhaji Abubakar asked. "Which hospital did you take him to?"

"He fell into the gutter," said Bilkisu, "and Kabiru took him to Murtala Hospital."

Alhaji Abubakar dressed quickly and left for the hospital, but he failed to find the patient there. One of the staff explained to him that the patient had been given an injection and sent back home. The caller then went to Alhaji Abdu's house where he found him being walked home in the arms of helpful neighbours. But when Alhaji Abubakar tried to greet him, he didn't respond immediately; he still seemed groggy, only half-conscious. So Alhaji Abubakar asked them not to take him inside, but to take him to a different hospital instead. He drove him to Nassarawa Hospital.

After the formalities of buying and filling out a registration card, he was seen by a doctor. The doctor detained the patient after Alhaji Abubakar paid the deposit. Alhaji Abdu was soon lying in a bed while nurses attended to him, giving him injections and cleaning his wounds. He received a prescription for the medicines that weren't immediately available. They didn't finish with him until sunset, when he fell asleep. Alhaji Abubakar left with Sani, while Kabiru stayed with the sick man.

The doctor diagnosed high blood pressure, and said that it was lucky they had brought the patient back to the hospital. If they hadn't, he said, he could have died.

Saudatu's husband drove her to Rabi's place at eight o'clock. "What happened to father?" Saudatu asked her mother. "What made him fall down? Did it happen here in the house?"

Rabi quickly related the story, though she left out the detail of having sent her husband unceremoniously on his way. She just said he had come and exchanged greetings with her and later left, after which Sani had come in and told them about the fall, and they had taken him out of the gutter and admitted him to the hospital.

"It was Alhaji Abubakar who took him to Nassarawa Hospital," said Saudatu.

"Yes, Sani said so."

"Let us go, Baba. My husband must be getting anxious waiting for us."

They bumped into him on the way out; he was on his way in to hurry them up. They got in the car and drove in silence until they reached the hospital. Alhaji Abubakar followed the women in, carrying the food, as Saudatu was too upset to do so, and it wouldn't have been respectful to let his mother-in-law carry it herself. They found the

patient with his face swollen. He tried to sit up when he
heard them come in, but Kabiru pressed him back down
to keep him from bringing on another headache.

It had been almost a year since Saudatu had seen her
father last, on the day he had sent them away from his
house. And of course it had been just as long since he
had seen her. He was surprised, then, to see how plump
and radiant she had become. She knelt and greeted him,
and her husband did so as well. Rabi simply stood by, not
saying anything to him. Alhaji Abubakar called Kabiru
aside, leaving Rabi and Saudatu with the patient, to ask
him what the doctor had said during his absence.

"Why not sit down?" Alhaji Abdu asked his wife and
daughter, speaking with difficulty. "You must be uncom-
fortable, to remain standing for long."

The women suddenly realized that he was crying as he
spoke to them.

"Why are you crying like a child?" Rabi scolded him.
"Don't you know that Saudatu's husband is close by?"

As if on cue, Alhaji Abubakar and Kabiru came in.
They stopped in mid-stride when they saw the patient
crying. Kabiru went over to him and said, "The doctor
asked you not to get too worked up..."

"But I must cry," the patient interrupted him.
"Whatever has happened to me, I brought it down on my
own head. Sin is like a puppy: if you stop and play with it
in the road, it will follow you home. Look at you, coming
here to see me in this state. One's relative always stays
close to him, no matter how far he falls. For God's sake,
forgive me, so that if I die now, I may be absolved some
of my sins."

All the people standing around the bed shed tears.
Saudatu cried the hardest of them all. After a long silence,
Rabi said to the patient, "We want to be on our way. May
you get well soon."

She left the room before he could wipe away his tears and respond to her.

"I want to go home, father," said Saudatu. "God willing, I will call again tomorrow in the evening."

"Thank you, Saudatu. May Allah bless you. Look after your husband well: he is a gentleman. May Allah bless you all. Thank you both."

"I will bring you food in the morning," said Alhaji Abubakar. "Let Sani stay here with you, since he doesn't have to go to school until the afternoon. Kabiru can go to the university tomorrow morning and come afterwards."

"All right, Alhaji," said Kabiru after a brief pause. "Thank you and good night."

Alhaji Abdu stayed in the hospital for eight days, during which time he received many visits from the relatives of Rabi and Alhaji Abubakar. He ate three square meals a day, prepared in the house of his son-in-law. Delicious dishes were sent regularly and on time, not to mention the other get-well gifts his visitors left him, like oranges and bananas. Alhaji Barau gave him fifty naira to pay for his medicine. His relatives, and Rabi's too, implored Rabi to go back to her husband's house. They refused to listen to anything she said in protest; they just wanted her to agree to go back.

She became so frustrated with their insistence that she stopped visiting him, until finally he was discharged from the hospital. Her son-in-law heard about her refusal and called on her after he had taken the patient home. She spread a mat for him, and after they exchanged greetings, he told her, "Baba has been discharged, and I have taken him and Sani home. The house is a mess and there is no one in it. Saudatu has told me everything that happened. They all want you to go back. Life is full of unhappiness, but we have to be understanding. Since he has admitted his mistake, you should go back to his house."

"I will not go back," she said. "He's already sent many others to beg me. He must be close to giving up, otherwise he wouldn't have asked you to come. Honestly Alhaji, I don't intend to ever go back there."

"For the sake of Allah and His Prophet, consider the interests of your children. Saudatu is very upset about it. Her father himself deserves some sympathy. I will ask Malam Shehu to collect people and renew your marital knot."

Rabi was at a loss. She couldn't argue with her son-in-law. Still, she started to object.

"Don't say anything," he stopped her. "For the sake of Allah, try to be understanding. What good is it living all by yourself? It's time to forgive and forget. I should be on my way, now."

Rabi watched him go. She didn't want to go to her brother's house and risk bumping into her son-in-law again. She couldn't very well leave town, either. Where would she go? She made up her mind to maintain her stance if her brother asked her about going back. She waited, but when he didn't turn up she decided to visit him and tell him herself. Just then an acquaintance of hers called to commiserate with her about Alhaji Abdu's illness, and overstayed. Finally Rabi made an excuse about an errand she had to run, and they parted.

As Rabi approached her brother's house, she saw several people walking away from it. Among them was Alhaji Abubakar, getting into his car. Then she saw Alhaji Bello about to ride away on his motorcycle, and he caught sight of her as well. She approached him uneasily, and he said to her teasingly, "Aha, here comes the bride! Welcome."

"Just *who* are you calling *bride*, Alhaji Bello?!" said Rabi indignantly. She felt like a young girl in a forced marriage. Inside her brother's house, she wept. He tried to reason with her, but eventually he had to give up. He told her that the people who had gathered there were unanimously in favour of her returning to her former husband's house. Her son-in-law had offered to foot the bill for the gifts and the kola nuts distributed at the event. Malam Shehu and Alhaji Bello had already informed the imam and the muezzin and began to make preparations. As for Alhaji Abdu, he wouldn't dare divorce Rabi again even if he were to be bitten by a rabid dog.

She left the house towards midnight without saying farewell to the family.

The next day, Alhaji Abubakar called on Rabi and presented her with four atamfa cloths and the sum of one hundred naira. Once again, he implored her to be understanding, and asked her what else it would take for her to agree go back to her husband's house, whether there was anything more she wanted.

"No, I don't want anything else," she said. "I've had enough of this. You can leave me alone now."

It took another twenty days, but in the end she gave in. Tasidi talked her into buying some furnishings—vinyl and curtains—and serving dishes. Saudatu, Tasidi and the wives of Malam Shehu and Alhaji Bello conveyed the bride to the house. Alhaji Abubakar donated one sack each of corn, rice, and maize, along with one hundred naira to buy daily provisions. He promised to open a new stall for Alhaji Abdu once he had fully recuperated from his affliction.

Rabi continued with her food-selling business. She could always be found attending to customers.

In the past, Alhaji Abdu had been the head of his household. But now everything had changed. He had trampled on the rights of those whose welfare Allah had entrusted to him, and he had fallen into ruin. Rabi now took over the role. She was the one who handed out the day's provisions, who distributed the detergent and soap.

She was the one responsible for giving the house a lick of paint when needed, and deciding what should go where.

Three months after the reconciliation, Saudatu gave birth to a beautiful baby boy. It was a crowning joy for her and her husband. Rabi had attended to Saudatu, going back and forth between the houses, until her delivery. But even afterwards, Saudatu's husband refused to let his wife go back home to undergo the forty-day bathing regimen because of all the other children she was looking after. It thus fell on Rabi to go every day and take her daughter through the bathing ritual. The baby was named Abdullahi, after Saudatu's father.

Alhaji Abubakar opened a new stall at Kwari Market, filled it with merchandise, and turned it over to Alhaji Abdu. Though everything was on loan, he could run the business as if it were his.

Alhaji Abdu's new life was something like the life of a dog in paradise: no trouble, but not much joy. Still, the Almighty had at last made it possible for him to know and seek the truth, and to turn away from falsehood.

THE END